Fa
Profe
Mi

Debbie Spencer

BlueRose ONE.com
Stories Matter

First Published in December 2022

ISBN: 978-93-5668-086-9

eISBN: 978-93-5668-087-6

BLUEROSE PUBLISHERS

www.BlueRoseONE.com
info@bluerosepublishers.com
+91 8882 898 898

Cover Design:
Muskan Sachdeva

Typographic Design:
Pooja Sharma

Distributed by: BlueRose, Amazon, Flipkart

Chapter One

Well my story starts with a theory, that will be explained more, as you carry on reading. Diana never really had any confidence, but finds the older she gets and the more wisdom that comes with age, finally she feels like she can do anything she puts her mind to. Diana mum of two children. A girl named Gabriel aged 19, extremely stunning but doesn't know it and very clever. A boy named Cameron aged 17, coming up to his 18th birthday in November 2022, who is very handsome, tough, extremely confident and very clever too. Diana also had a beautiful Labrador named Leo, age 3, going to be 4 on the 22nd May 2022. He is so adorable and very clever, but has not fulfilled his potential due to Diana's illness which will all become clear as you carry on reading. Diana was bed bound for five years due to no fault of her own. When Diana's husband Tony first got Leo., Tony and Cameron took him training. He was so clever, the trainers never used to get him up to show the rest of the class a training activity so one day Tony asked, "Why do you never get Leo up?" The trainer who was called Isobel said, "Because Leo just picks it up too easily, and we just need to get the pups up who struggle more."

Diana, the Mum, who lost her way because she never had enough confidence to fulfil her dreams. Diana was so beautiful and worked in a grocery shop. Customers would comment "What on earth are you working here for? You could be a Model." However Diana never saw herself like that due to being bullied at school. Kids could be so cruel and don't realise the damage they can do psychologically! One kid just commented one day, saying "Doesn't Diana remind you of a monkey?!" All the kids started laughing and from that moment Diana's nickname was monkey. The kids used to also be violent with Diana, she made the mistake of hanging around with kids that Diana was nothing like. Yvonne was Diana's best friend in school, she used to say how pretty Diana was and how she had big beautiful blue eyes and would always say how she wished she could look like her, but when they were at school with all the other kids, she'd be so different because she just went along with Karen who was one of their other friends and the cock of the school.

Diana used to hang around at home with Andrea, Sarah, Micky, Joanne, Lisa and Marne. They were all at Marne's house and got very, very drunk! Diana had never had alcohol before, but showing off downed nearly a full bottle of whiskey, so you can imagine how drunk she was! She could hardly walk so they all went outside to get her some fresh air and Diana never shut up talking and doing daft things to make them all laugh. Then they went to Joanne's house and her brother Paul was in. Paul is also famous but I can't tell you what for, as you will recognise him straight away. Well poor Paul, Diana starts dancing and stripping off, trying to get Paul to dance with her but Paul was running away, so Diana was chasing him around the sofa. It was funny at the time and oh so innocent. Diana's best friend was Andrea. She was so tough but never a bully, she was as hard as Karen, but a lot nicer and friendly. They used to do everything together, but Diana's biggest mistake she ever made was falling out with her over something so stupid! That's how she became closer to Yvonne, which she regretted for a very long time, but they really got on well. Even though Diana was a shy, extremely kind and soft girl, Yvonne was totally the opposite, that's probably why they got on so well. All the girls did what Karen said, because they just wanted to fit in with her and be as cool as she was. If you were in Karen's gang, you were in the in crowd she was a very hard and extremely cruel girl. Everything Karen said, the girls did, probably because they were scared of her. As gentle as Diana was she wasn't scared or didn't take orders from anyone. She had her own mind and was a very strong minded girl and therefore never fitted in with Karen or the other girls. She only was friends with them because Yvonne wanted to be as cool as them all. Diana just wanted to do well in school and work hard, but they made it difficult for her. Karen didn't particularly like Diana, because she couldn't control her.

One day Karen said to Yvonne, "I've no idea why you're friends with Diana, she calls you behind your back. One of the girls called Tracey didn't like Yvonne. She thought she was a lesbian. Yvonne invited all the girls back to her house for a sleepover except Tracey and Lisa. Lisa was very close to Tracey, (they were like two peas in a pod) when Tracey found out she wasn't very happy that her and Lisa hadn't been invited. Tracey decided to get her own back by spreading rumours about Yvonne trying it on with Angela and trying to get Diana involved too, but Diana went home. Tracey liked Diana, thought she was a nice girl and didn't want to get her involved.

Karen saw her opportunity to get Yvonne and Diana to fight. Karen went on to say, "Yvonne, remember when that rumour went around school about you being a lesbian? It was Diana who started it. Ask everyone if you want. Well obviously all the girls weren't going to go against Karen, as much as they liked Diana. Yvonne was fuming! It was all so childish, but that is girls for you. Yvonne pulled Diana up and they argued and fell out. Karen thought I'll get closer to Yvonne, while they're not friends. Karen started to make a big fuss of Yvonne. Yvonne obviously liked the attention she was getting from Karen, it was like a dream come true for her. Then Karen genuinely started to like Yvonne, the closer they got. One day Karen said to Yvonne, "don't you think, we're getting a lot closer than the other girls." Yvonne genuinely said, "Well yes I've been thinking about you and me for a while, I definitely can see us getting closer." Karen unlike herself thought yes me too. Then bringing herself back to reality, thought yes this is absolutely what I set out to achieve. But feeling a bit bad for using Yvonne. Thought ahh well, it can't do any harm. Surprising herself thought, "I really do want to be best friends with Yvonne" and because she was the more dominant of the two. Eventually made this reality.

Yvonne genuinely found herself getting closer to Karen and sadly remembered how close she and Diana had once been, so before she could change her own mind apologises to Diana for the false accusations. Diana too was very happy, that Yvonne had apologised. So believe it or not, they both became friends again. After Diana going to Yvonne saying, "I am sorry too, we were both in the wrong," and they quickly began to get back to where they were.

Karen seeing this, began to get jealous, even though they still involved her, but Karen wasn't happy to share, she just wanted Yvonne all to herself. Karen was an extremely selfish, controlling, mean and jealous girl and when she didn't get her own way troubles would start. So Karen, started to plot her next move, she really needed to get them to fight. She started with coming up with a lie that was going to get Yvonne want to fight Diana. She told Yvonne, "Yvonne have you seen what

Diana has wrote about you in bubble writing." She had wrote in massive letters, Yvonne is a slag. She thinks she can have any boy she wants. Diana and Yvonne both fancied the same lad Anthony, but Yvonne having more confidence than Diana asked Anthony out and he said yes. Diana was a bit upset at first, but not enough to write these nasty words, she just wasn't like that. So Karen showing Yvonne this, made her blood boil. So when Karen suggested that Yvonne should challenge Diana to a fight she didn't really think about it and just went straight to Diana and offered her out after school. Diana in shock said "Yvonne, I don't really want to fight you over a lad. I don't like him that much to throw our friendship away."

Anyway the more Yvonne thought about it, when she'd calmed down the more it didn't make sense to her. She knew deep down that Diana wasn't really like that, but couldn't think of anyone else who would do it either. Yvonne approached Diana, and said "when we're supposed to meet at the shop after school, don't turn up. So Karen will know you don't want to fight me." Diana replied, "No problem Yvonne, I won't show up, but if I get dragged there by all the girls, will you promise me that you'll tell Karen you don't want to fight me either." So they both shook on it. Now waiting patiently, Diana thought to herself, "I don't 100% trust Yvonne, so what do I do about it!? Diana wasn't stupid, so said to herself I'm just going wait and see what happens next.

Karen told Yvonne to start a fight with Diana, but Yvonne didn't want to, so she approached Diana and said, "Diana, Karen wants us to fight after school at the top shop. But I don't want to, but don't want to look scared. So can you just tell the teacher about it," Diana said, "No I'm not grassing, why don't you? I don't want to look scared either." Home time comes, and Diana feeling a bit anxious. Walking to the school gates, she sees them all waiting outside the shop. She can either run back into the school, or go and face her fears. Diana was a very brave girl, and never backed down to anyone. Have you ever got that sinking feeling in your stomach?!? That's what Diana was feeling, but she carried on walking towards them all.

Chapter Two

Yvonne was looking nervous too, but she had Karen to back her up, and obviously the rest of the girls just do what Karen says. Yvonne walks over to Diana and acting hard says "I want a fight!" Diana says ok whatever. So Yvonne pulls her hair, and Diana's reaction is to just pull her hair back, and then their throwing punches at each other. Diana is quite a bit taller than Yvonne, so is getting the better of her, Karen seeing this. Starts to get involved and so do the other girls except Tracey and Lisa, they just stand back watching! Karen pulling out an egg...eggs Diana and all the other girls start kicking and punching Diana! Diana thinks to herself, don't cry the girls get more violent, and start kicking her in the head. Diana thinking to herself, if I don't cry. They could really do some damage. So Diana starts crying, and luckily there's an older man coming out of the shop and drags all the girls off Diana. And says to her go and run home.

Diana runs into her house, and when her mum sees her, concerningly runs over to her and says, "who on earth has done this to you? Diana said, "Me and Yvonne were fighting, and then someone eggs me and they all jump on me pulling my hair, punching and kicking me in the head first then everywhere until a guy pulls them off me. Tells me to run home. So her mum fuming! Goes to the house closest to them which is Tracey's. Bangs on the door, shouting! "You should see what your daughter and the rest of them have done to Diana!" Well Tracey's parents have always loved Diana, and can't believe it. They are really ashamed of Tracey, and ground her for a month. The bad thing is, Diana's mum didn't know where the rest of them lived, so they all get away with it. Tracey wasn't happy especially because she and Lisa didn't get involved!

Back at school, Tracey wasn't feeling very happy with Diana. So when Tracey and Lisa used to stick up for Diana, the dynamics of the group had totally changed. Karen started to like Diana more, and started making a fuss of her. Karen invited Diana round for tea.

Diana wasn't sure what was going on. But soon it became the norm. Karen and Diana were getting really close, Karen wondering why she never liked Diana?!? Because now they were becoming best friends. Yvonne started getting a bit jealous. They were no longer best friends, Yvonne started to wonder why she had even loved Diana, and Diana felt the same about Yvonne. Yvonne made a good friend, but when you have her as an enemy, it was lethal. But Diana wasn't bothered. Karen kept telling her, "you got the better of her anyway, so don't worry about her." Meanwhile Diana was starting to love school again, and had no worries or fears of anyone. The more Yvonne watched Karen and Diana, the more jealous she'd get. But obviously she wouldn't go against the cock of the school. But thought to herself, I may not be able to do anything about it in the playground, but I can in the classroom. Especially in English, when Diana and Yvonne had that lesson together only.

Yvonne used to try stirring it to the teacher, when anything would go wrong in the classroom. Yvonne used to always blame it on Diana. Until one day Diana snapped! And grabbing Yvonne in front of the teacher, smashed her head onto the table. The teacher sent Diana to the headteacher.

Diana was in a lot of trouble, more than she'd ever been. Headteacher was very surprised to see Diana! She said, "I'm surprised at you Diana! What was all that about?" Diana replied, "Yvonne just pushed me too far, everything that goes wrong in the classroom, Yvonne lies to the teacher, saying Diana done it, I just had enough of her lies. And me being punished for it!"

Headteacher replies "yes but that is part of life, you can't go around smashing everyone's head in. So for your punishment. You're going to say sorry to Yvonne." Diana replies, "Yes I understand that, but will you get Yvonne to apologise to me for telling lies about me please." Teacher says, "No, because we've got no proof of her lying." Diana shocked! Raises her voice a bit "but I'm no liar! I always tell the truth!" Head teacher says, "Don't raise your voice to me. Show some Respect! For that, you're going to stay behind tonight and write some lines, I will not raise my voice to the headteacher again. And I am very sorry." Diana replies, "Ok I will do that, because I am very sorry and I've always shown respect to all the teachers." Diana goes to detention, and does her lines calmly. She also adds at the end, I am so sorry for showing disrespect to the headteacher, it's not like me. I am always so respectful to my elders. I apologise profusely.

When Karen hears about this, she is not happy about it! Pulling Yvonne says, "Yvonne I want you to apologise to Diana now!" So Yvonne does. And that's the end of that. Well you think it's the end, but Karen not long after. Breaks her leg, fighting with some older girls and all chase her down a hill. Karen running down the hill, falls and tumbles down. The older girls just laugh and leave her there.

So Karen being in hospital, for a couple of weeks. Gives Yvonne the opportunity to start stirring with the other girls, lying says, "Diana now thinks she is the cock of the school, while Karen is in hospital. I think we should show her that she is getting too big for her boots. What do you all reckon? I think we should all wait for her at the top shop and jump her." Some of the girls agreed, that included Tracey and Lisa. Because they didn't stick up for her anymore. And the others didn't want to get involved.

So Diana walking home, sees all the girls waiting outside the shop all the girls start shouting "get her, we'll show her who's boss while Karen's away." So they egg her again, pull her hair and start kicking and punching Diana and dragging her around the floor, throwing stones at her, they call her, "monkey over and over again!" When Karen gets out of the hospital. She is not very happy with Yvonne, Tracey, and a few of the others who got involved beating Diana up. So when back in school, says to them. "Who wants to fight Diana on your own?" Tracey said, "I will no problem." So they fight but no one wins, but Diana has to admit to herself that when Tracey punched her in her head, it really hurt! But because she didn't like to show emotion, when somebody hurt her. She never told anyone that Tracey hurt her even more than when they all jumped her. So when everyone said, "that Diana and Tracey drawn." Diana thought to herself. I wouldn't like to fight Tracey again, she's really hard. So when it came to Tracey wanting to fight Yvonne. Because she blamed Yvonne for herself and Diana not being as close as they once were. Yvonne went to Diana and said, "Diana what was Tracey like to fight?" Diana could tell that Yvonne was really scared and says, "She's tough, she really hurt me and to be honest I don't think you stand a chance against her." Diana smiling to herself could tell that Yvonne was so scared! But thought ahh well she deserves it. Anyway everyone stood around watching them fight. Could tell that Tracey got the best of Yvonne. And Diana thought nice one she deserves it. So Diana goes over to Tracey to say, "Nice one Tracey. You well got the better of her. And I'm just so gutted we're not close anymore. You know I never told my mum. Who it was who jumped me, "I only told her about me fighting Yvonne, and then someone eggs me and all joined in and started kicking and punching me!" So Tracey says, "so how come she only came around to my house? I got proper shouted at for that and grounded for a month. I was fuming with you, that's why I am not the same with you anymore." So Diana says, "Because yours is the only house my mum knew. I am so sorry for that." Tracey says, "Ok I am so sorry too then. I really thought you'd told your mum that I joined in too. So you can imagine why I was so angry with you, seeing as though Lisa and I were the only ones who didn't join in."

Chapter Three

You could say, Diana getting multiple sclerosis was a Blessing in disguise, which will all become clearer the more you read. She developed M.S when she was 32, after having 2nd Child Cameron. It started with blurred vision, which she thought at first, was a Migraine. But it lasted too long, to be a migraine. So She went to the doctors, who referred her to the Eye Clinic (who were a total waste of time), Diana had to argue with them! To finally get them to listen to her which only exacerbated Symptoms and caused stress and anxiety.

Nellie, Diana's mum had died of a brain tumour. When she was 55 and Diana was 19. She was left devastated! But always remembered what the Amazing Nurses told her, they said "if you ever have a long, reoccurring headache that just won't go. Make sure, you demand a brain scan." Which is exactly what Diana did. The thing is, Diana was respectful and always looked up to the professionals, thought they were better than her. Well how she learnt the hard way. That no one is better than you, and no one is worse than you. (Which she never thought she was better than anyone else anyway.) So the moral of the story is. Doesn't matter if you're a Consultant or homeless no one is better than anyone. Always remember that!

At hospital Diana was passed from Pilar to post. Doctors were trying to tell her she was suffering from a different kind of migraine. Diana wasn't having any of it. Eventually she'd had enough! So snapped! Demanding a brain scan! Well they were humming and aahing started questioning like "is there anyone in your family, who suffers with Multiple sclerosis? Or any other brain conditions?" Diana told them, "My mum died from a Brain Tumour." So they went away discussing with the other Doctors. Now she realised they were suspecting something. But never crossed her mind, it was Multiple sclerosis. She was thinking it was worse than that like brain cancer. Anyway she overheard heard doctors discussing money. So suspected that's what it had all been about all along. Which made her furious! She sat down, and angrily said, "I'm not budging until I get a brain scan!" Anyway it worked, to cut a long story short. Diana had a brain scan, and it took 6 weeks to get the results back. Eventually it's time to go Hospital and get results. Feeling nervous and anxious. Diana went on her own, as Tony was busy at work. Which never bothered her. Diana had learnt to be brave and walk alone in life.

When her mum died, Diana didn't feel like she could go on without her. So sadly she tried to kill herself, by taking a lot of paracetamol. Fell asleep and then just woke up. At the time Diana wasn't very happy. That she just woke up, but now feeling very thankful that it wasn't meant to be. But Diana felt ill for a full week afterwards and really sickly. So I really don't think taking a full pack of paracetamol is the answer, and believe me when I tell you, it's not the easy way out as well. And could be one of the reasons why Diana has Multiple Sclerosis. Diana had 2 sisters who were older than her, the Eldest sister Jasmine was 8years older and middle sister Kelsey was 7 years older than Diana, she loved her family life when she was young. She had the perfect mum, who was like a God to her. All her friends wanted her Mum to be their mum. Diana felt like the luckiest girl in the world. Because she was the youngest. Her mum and Auntie Mo (Maureen) used to call her princess, and she was treated like one as well. Her home life was perfect, and all of the three children. Knew they were loved so much. Those were the happy days. Diana thought, "Wish I could say the same about my school life."

But no, that was far from perfect, it was the total opposite. She loved primary school, Diana was shy, but had lots of friends. Her best friend Kerry from the age of 8 years old, Kerry was also shy and still is Diana's best friend now at age 49. She loved her they are close but don't see each other every day. They can go for long periods of time without seeing each other, but when they get together again, it's just like they've not been apart, and can just pick up from where they left off. Diana had always been so friendly and kind so she had lots of friends.

Anyway when she got into High School, things went downhill drastically. I mean she got in with the wrong crowd. Sort of was friends with them in Primary School. But they were ok in primary school, they consisted of Karen (who was the cock of the school) Tracey who lived very close to her and always played out together and go back to each other's house. She was a plump girl with a very bubbly personality. And because Diana was shy but very friendly. They always got on very well. Then there was Andrea who was very pretty and popular with the other girls because she was so pretty. Francine who was a good fighter too, so Karen and Francine used to always fight over Andrea.

In primary school, which was called, 'All The Little Ones.' All the girls just mingled together. Diana was still really good friends with Kerry. But she wasn't in Diana's gang. Lucky for her, she was good friends with Lisa, Diana was too, but Lisa and Kerry just seemed to be together more. Because Diana was in this stupid gang. Diana shouldn't have been in really. Her boyfriend was called Jason who she met when they were 8 years old in primary school, he was a very popular boy, and all the girls fancied him, but he liked Diana the best out of all of them. Even Andrea, which really shocked Diana. Because she was the girl that was popular and pretty. But no, he always insisted Diana was the prettiest. In fact looking back, all the boys used to fancy Diana and you know what it's like in primary school. All the boys used to line up and Diana would kiss one at a time. All the kids used to play this game. Ha-ha and they thought they were the Bees knees. Bless their little cotton socks.

Then it all went downhill, when one kid said Diana reminded her of a monkey. Then that was it. Diana's nickname was monkey. Don't know if it was because she was always climbing trees. Who knows, but she hated being called monkey. Kids can be so cruel. Diana remembered this really pretty blonde haired girl, and someone said she reminded them of a frog, and then that was it. Yes, her nickname was froggy. She didn't deserve it because she was so pretty. Anyway I'll get back to my story.

Chapter Four

Diana's mum was her world, and she lived on her own with her mum. And Auntie Mo used to come around a lot, she was at Diana's birth and always treated her like she was hers. So they were very close.

Like I said Diana was a young 19 and very spoilt. She didn't even know how to cook or anything, because her mum did everything for her. She said, "Her time will come to do all those things. While you are young, you should be playing out and having fun."

You see Diana's mum Nellie, never really had much of a childhood. She was born in 1937, one of 6 children. Nellie was the oldest girl and had same name as her mum, then there were May, Tommy (same name as his Dad because he was born first) who died as a baby, John, Eddie, Jimmy died at the young age of 21 after he was happily married as well. He died of TB, and because their mum wanted to be close to him and take care of him, she also catches it. Jimmy died which broke their mum's heart. She was never the same after that. Jimmy was her favourite, because he was her first born. It wasn't long after, sadly she passed away of TB too, leaving 4 children behind. Their dad who was called Tommy was in the Navy at War. He had to be released to raise the children. He was suffering from the aftermath of the war. Which we call PTSD now. But because in them days, they didn't believe anything was wrong with him. Doctors said it was just psychological. Wasn't long after he died. It was said, he died of a broken heart as he lost his wife who he loved dearly, and also his son

Jimmy who he thought the world of, was very proud of him, and so happy when he got married and was released for the day to give his son away. It was one of his happiest days.

Nellie was only a 13 years old child, but because she was the oldest girl. She had to finish school to look after the rest of the children. Who consisted of John 21, Eddie 17, May was only 9. John had to go out to work, while Nellie became a young Mum to take care of them all. By cooking, cleaning, basically the role of the Mum. It was a lot of stress and responsibility to put on young shoulders. Nellie was too much of a perfectionist. She did all this, while battling with her own issues. Nellie liked girls from the age of 7, she took after her mum because her mum also preferred girls. It wasn't easy being homosexual in them days. It was very hard for Nellie to admit her sexuality to everyone, and to herself as well. This is something she battled with most of her life. When Nellie was 21 she got married to a man called Jimmy. Who she never loved. Jimmy used to look like Elvis, so he was admired by many women, but he fell in love with Nellie. Nellie was so stressed out! Being in a loveless marriage. Then she became pregnant nine months later, she gives birth to a beautiful girl, named her jasmine. Nellie used to hate hospitals, so couldn't wait to get out. While Nellie was in hospital, Jimmy had bought a beautiful house in Middleton and done it all up for when Nellie came home with jasmine. Jimmy feeling excited went to pick his wife and new baby up from hospital. He couldn't wait for his wife to see it, well when Nellie walked into her new house she absolutely loved it, and hugged Jimmy saying, "thank you so much for this beautiful house." Nellie despite herself said, "I think we are going to be so happy here, new beginnings in our new house, which will become our home for ever." She was actually very happy for a long time.

Jimmy knew Nellie didn't love him deep down but he adored her. And was so happy with his new life, he didn't seem to care.

Life is good. Nellie and Jimmy are very happy. Nellie is so proud of Jasmine and puts everything into bringing her up, cooking and cleaning while. Jimmy goes to work. Nellie can sacrifice liking women, to be with Jimmy and their daughter Jasmine. Jasmine is her life and her world, she could do anything for Jasmine. She loved taking her out everywhere, and joined a mother and baby group. Where she met new friends with babies, and they all became good friends. There were Irene, Betty, Flo, and Marie, they used to take turns to invite each other back once a week, so when they didn't have a mother and baby group every Monday they would go round to Nellie's, then Irene's, everyone would take a turn every Monday. So every day of the week they were all busy and loved their lives.

Nellie started to feel sick and then was actually sick, so her friends said, "you should go and get a pregnancy test." Nellie rang doctors to get an appointment with Dr Walker, her favourite doctor. Nellie went to her appointment with jasmine and had a pregnancy test. When she got the results back. It was positive, Nellie didn't know how to feel, on one hand she was happy and on the other, she was anxious. Not sure if they could afford to have a second baby. But Jimmy was made up when he heard this great news. He said, "Don't worry my darling, we will be ok with two children, don't you worry about that." So Nellie felt a lot better about having a baby now. She started to enjoy her pregnancy again, because she loved knowing that there's a little life growing inside her. Nellie was a very tough lady, but hated violence! The only time she would fight is to protect herself or others. If she seen someone being bullied, she would jump in and batter them. Nellie was a genuine, lovely woman, everyone who knew her loved her.

Chapter Five

So the story goes, Nellie had to still take Jasmine to the play group, which she really enjoyed, it was a good job it was in the afternoon. Because she still had morning sickness, was wondering, how long is this sickness going to last for. She never suffered with it, with jasmine. But so glad she felt better in the afternoon, because she loved taking jasmine to the mother and baby group. On the other days, her friends would have everyone over, and said to Nellie, you don't have to while you're pregnant.

Nellie and her friends were chatting about being married and how much they loved it, but Nellie didn't comment. Her friends said, "Nellie you have gone quiet," Nellie replied just saying, "I love my Jimmy, but there are times, I just need a break from him." Her friend Flo said, "I know how you feel. Would you like to go somewhere for the weekend like Blackpool or something." Nellie quickly said "I would love to." So they arranged to go to a hotel for the weekend. Jimmy looked after jasmine for the weekend, and said to Nellie, "You go and have a nice rest." So Nellie and Flo walked into their room in the hotel, and it was lovely. After a little while Flo said, "Nellie have you ever kissed a girl?" Nellie surprised said, "No but to tell the truth, I do like girls, I would rather be with a woman than a man, but life has got in the way of that." Flo said, "I had a feeling you were into women like me." Nellie feeling happy just kissed Flo and one thing led to another, then they were naked fondling each other. Nellie was in heaven, she never dreamed this would happen. Flo had done this before, so took the lead, the next thing they were having sex. They both were so excited and came together. But they didn't want to stop, so Flo started kissing Nellie all over her body and went down on her until she had the biggest orgasm she had ever had in her life. Nellie returned the same to Flo and Flo was screaming in pleasure. They both just lay there cuddling. Then don't stop making love to each other until they become really tired. So having a nice sleep. When they awoke, they both looked at each other and just decided to stay in bed all day, and make love until early hours in the morning. The next day, they woke up and decided to stay in bed and make love all day again. In fact for the whole weekend they just stayed in bed making love. They never wanted the weekend to end, but all good things have to come to an end. Anyway it was time to go back to reality. Nellie and Flo had the time of their lives.

Nellie feeling very guilty, walks into her home, and the first thing she does is pick jasmine up and tells her how much she loves her and how much she had missed her. Jimmy asks, did you have a good time?" Nellie replied, It was just what I needed" Nellie knew from this point onwards, she could give everything to her family. But she couldn't stop thinking about Flo. But knew she had to put her to the back of her mind. Anyway she carries on going to the mother and baby group. Seeing Flo, she tells her, "I can't see you anymore as much as I would love to. I'm so sorry, I have to focus on my family and getting prepared for labour." Nellie only had 3 months to go before she meets her baby, Jimmy and Nellie were very excited to be meeting their baby soon. Thinking well if we have a girl again, at least we have jasmine's baby clothes. But if we have a boy, thinking we should go and buy a few new baby clothes in neutral colours, and a little something for jasmine too so she doesn't feel left out.

Nine months has passed and Nellie is due to go into hospital. In the hospital Nellie is having her check-up, when she starts to go into labour, she doesn't want the epidural, but asks for some gas and air. Nellie is an extremely brave woman, and can deal with pain very well. She starts getting contractions and is breathing into each contraction, controlling the pain as best she can. 12 hours later she gives birth to a baby girl. Oh she's overwhelmed again and names her new baby Kelsey. Jimmy is so overwhelmed with his little family and says, "Nellie I love our family and can't wait to get you both home safely to our beautiful home.

So she walks into her house and is so glad to be home. Jasmine is really clinging to her mum Nellie says, "Jasmine it's ok, I have enough love for you both, meet Kelsey your sister." "No I don't want a sister," says jasmine. Nellie starts laughing, "Well there's nothing I can do about that now, don't worry jasmine my beautiful little girl. I love you both the same so much." For the next week or so, jasmine is really playing up, shouting! "I don't want a sister, it's not fair." Nellie thinking to herself just give it time and everything will be ok.

Meanwhile Flo, is plotting her revenge. Nellie has had the baby now, so she should be with me. She goes to the house knocking on the door, or should I say banging on the door! Nellie opening the door, is shocked to see Flo. She says "oh I'm sorry I've not been in touch with you, but I did tell you I don't want to see you anymore." Flo says, "as if it's that easy Hey, I want to speak with Jimmy." So Nellie slamming the door on her. Thinking oh well I didn't expect that from Flo.

Meanwhile Flo finds out where Jimmy's works is, and going to confront him, tells everything about her and Nellie.

Jimmy thinking to himself, well I always knew deep down that Nellie didn't love me and now I know why. I have to find out if this is true what Flo's told me. Feeling used, confronts Nellie saying, "Is this true what Flo has told me about you and her in bed for the whole weekend making love." Nellie says, "Yes I am so sorry Jimmy, but I've always liked girls more since I was age 7." Jimmy snapping, "Then what on earth are you doing with me? Is it just because we have jasmine together and now Kelsey." Nellie replies, "Well sadly it is the reason we are a family now and I've been trying to forget about women. But it is really hard to be something you're not. When all I really want is to be with a woman." Jimmy snaps and says angrily, "well go and be with Flo if that's what you want?!?!" But Nellie no longer wants to be with Flo. Anyway Jimmy moves out, leaving the house to Nellie and their children.

Years and years later when Diana was in her late twenties, twenty eight to be more precise, Diana was living in Ashton in Makerfield when she received a letter, saying that her uncle John had sadly passed away, and left some money to her. The thing is John dies of cancer and in his will, he leaves all his money to his siblings. Like Eddie, Nellie and May, but because Nellie had died, it was split out between all Nellie's daughters like Jasmine, Kelsey and Diana. Diana was sad to hear about her Uncle John because she had always loved him. Then she heard about her Uncle Eddie had also died but he just left all his money and house to his sister May. Which didn't bother Diana because she had never met him anyway. He was a recluse so never went out of his house anyway to go and see people, he had also died of Cancer. So there was only May left, who Diana had met her a lot of times when growing up. The last time she seen her Auntie May was just before her sister Jasmine died. Diana and Jasmine had been invited to their Cousin Julie's 50th birthday party. Sadly that was the last time Diana had been out with Jasmine, because Diana not long after that became bed bound with Chronic Fatigue. Worst time of Diana and her family's life. Diana couldn't even go to her sister's funeral, which really upset Diana. But Tony took Gabriel and Cameron, and Jasmine came to Diana in a dream, which felt so real to say she loved her and totally understood why she couldn't make it.

Chapter Six

Diana is so happy with her husband Tony and two children. But thinking now the children are older, I can go out to work, she thinks well I could be a psychologist or social worker. She gets an opportunity to be a social worker. So goes for that, looking after children, but thinks to herself, the safety of children needs sorting out. We need to make sure the rules are changed because it's not good enough. All these children that are being let down by their parents, and the social workers to be honest.

So Diana has a word with her boss. Her boss totally agrees with Diana, but we need to raise a lot of money. So that is what they do, thinking of ways to raise money, a social worker comes up with, "Why don't we have lots of coffee mornings." Diana and the others agree, but after a while doing coffee mornings just isn't making enough money, they were all trying to think of something else to do as well. Kathleen says, "I don't know how you will all feel about this, but to make big money. We could give selling drugs for my cousin Graham ago?" Diana says, "Oh I'm not sure about that." But they all take a vote on it, and the selling drugs wins.

So they give it a go. They're making a lot more money than they were having coffee mornings. A lot more money. Diana is still not 100% sure about it. Anyway she meets Graham, and when Graham sees Diana he falls in love at first sight. He explains everything to Diana and puts her mind at ease. After that Graham keeps going to see Diana, asking her out on a date? But Diana tells him she is happily married, but Graham won't give up, he is also a bouncer at a night club, and says he can get them all in for free, the nightclub also has somewhere for them all to sleep too.

Graham won't give up, asking Diana on a date. Diana just keeps telling him no. Anyway they all decide to try this nightclub out. They're having such a great time. Diana has never danced so much, something Diana is really good at, and gets so much male attention. Graham is just watching Diana all night, then eventually strutting over to her, whisks her around the dance floor. Diana is laughing a lot, is quite drunk at this point. Graham takes total advantage and starts kissing Diana, he is telling her, "you are so beautiful, your husband is such a lucky man." Diana is feeling very flattered and happily says, "thank you Graham, you're a gorgeous looking man yourself. Just that I've never been unfaithful to Tony."

Well the night just gets better and Graham says to Diana, "I wish I could take you somewhere we can be alone for the night." Well Diana unlike herself says, "Where do you want to take me?" Graham getting excited says, "Diana I just want to make love to you all night?" Graham taking Diana by the hand takes her to one of the bedrooms, kissing her all over her body and telling her how much he wants her. She starts getting a bit excited herself, telling Graham, ok I'm yours, "What do you want to do to me" Graham just slowly taking Diana over to the bed, kisses her everywhere. Until they fall onto the bed, Graham quickly putting on a condom, carries on kissing her all the way down. Diana starts breathing really heavy and moaning don't stop. Which makes Graham even more excited, losing control he takes her roughly and takes her and his own clothes off quickly. He can't believe how much he wants her, "Diana I've never felt like this about anyone, I just want to do everything to you." Diana says, "For tonight only you can do anything you want to me." So there's no more talking just heavy breathing and moaning loudly.

Chapter Seven

Waking up the next morning, Diana is feeling really guilty on Tony and says, "Graham we can never do this again. This has just been a one off, I'm so sorry but I'm happily married." Graham says, "Ok but I really like you and it's not going to be that easy for me."

So Diana concentrating on looking out for the children, says, "Right now we've got enough money, we need to put it into action. Diana makes a list of the most vulnerable, and immediately starts helping them more straight away. We'll start by going through the list we have and make some check-up calls. I'll start with the babies and the younger children who are more at risk." So looking through the list of babies, makes Diana's blood boil. She has always been so passionate about babies and very young children. Thinking who on earth would want to hurt these vulnerable little babies and children. But she knows she has to keep it professional, as much as she would love to go round and give them a piece of her mind. She cannot do that. So she makes her first call to a 1 month old baby who is very vulnerable at the hands of the mum's boyfriend, who is known for child abuse. Diana knocks on the door, and says this is just a routine check-up call, to see how things are going. Can I please have a look around the house. The mother is very co-operative saying I am now on my own raising my baby. So Diana says, "Would it be okay for me to take a look around then please." The mother lets Diana in no problem. Everything looks fine and so happy to say the boyfriend has definitely gone.

Diana carries on these routines for months and happy to say everything is fine. As Diana's busy working, Graham is not giving up so easily, he sends flowers and chocolates to her, but Diana keeps telling him no. Graham getting a bit sick of it now, reminds Diana that he thinks so much of her and can't just forget her like that so easy, "Please let me take you out to somewhere really special." Diana finally giving in to Graham says, "Okay where are you going to take me then?" Graham feeling so happy surprises Diana by picking her up in a limousine. And taking her to the best restaurant, she has ever seen.

Graham leading Diana into the restaurant, Tells her, he thinks he's in love with her. Diana laughing tells him, "We've only slept together once." I know he says, "But I'm definitely in love with you, I can't stop thinking about you and I feel sick and gutted when you tell me you don't want to see me again. I can't eat or do anything else to make you see I'm so mad about you, please give me a chance to show you I'm for real." So Diana admitting, "Graham I feel something for you too. But I love my husband and my family life so much."

Diana just doesn't know what to do. Graham says, "I don't want to take you away from your family, just love to be able to see you too." Diana thinking about this, thinks I could do that. I could love them both and still be with my family. So that is what she does. Because it's new with Graham, she feels so much passion for him and wants to do everything too. Graham takes her by her hand, and leads her into his lovely house and says, "Diana my love, this is where we can explore our love, I want to make love to you all night, is there any way you can stay the night with me?" Diana thinking says, "not tonight but Tony is working away from tomorrow." So Graham feeling very excited can't wait for tomorrow to come.

Tomorrow is here, and Graham intends to make the most of it, getting really turned on and cannot wait to get started. He grabs Diana gently and leads her to his bed, thinking first I'm going to start with a massage with baby oil. He puts the oil all over Diana's back and starts rubbing it all in, starts the massage from her shoulders to her bottom, gets really carried away on her bottom and places one finger inside. Hearing Diana moaning, makes him want to make love to her. So he whispers, "can I get my vibrator, Diana you will love it. I'll use the vibration on your clit while putting my penis up your bum and the oil will make it easier to slide into you." Diana moans, "Yes that sounds good to me" Graham puts on a condom pushing himself into her, while Diana is moaning louder now! Shouting I'm going to come, so Graham says me too my love. They both orgasm together very loudly! Diana wanting more now, she can't get enough. So Graham turns her over and kissing her all over her body, makes his way down and all the way down until Diana is moaning I'm going to come again. He is getting really excited now putting on a condom, slides himself into her and they are both moaning together really loudly. Diana gasps, "this is amazing Graham! I never want you to stop." Graham says, "Don't worry my darling, we have all night." So the night is just beginning of making love all night long.

Chapter Eight

Back to reality and home life, Diana cannot stop thinking about Graham. Graham is back at work and can't stop thinking about Diana. So he decides to ring her and tell her how he feels about her. "Diana that was the best sex I have ever had. I'm more in love with you now. I didn't intend to fall madly in love with you, but I have. I want to be with you all the time." I know Diana says, "But we can't be together all of the time Graham, you know I love my husband and my children too much to ever leave them." Graham sighs, "Still even after last night, my love. I just am too much in love with you, I didn't mean for this to happen Diana." But Graham tries to stop thinking about Diana so much, out of respect for her and her family life, but he can't. He has fallen deeply in love with Diana.

Diana is back to work and is trying to get Graham out of her mind. I feel really bad on him, but what can I do, he knows I'm happily married and love my family too much to ever hurt them, I only met him in the first place to raise more funds to help the children. I love being a social worker to help vulnerable children and babies. Graham knows this and he also knows I am happily married. Why am I having to explain myself so much?!? And why do I feel really bad for Graham? She keeps asking herself over and over again, the truth is, she has fallen for him too. But getting on with her life is more important to her. Her husband Tony is a very good consultant in brain injuries and is one of the best in the country. Her daughter works in biomedical science at university and her son is doing a level maths and engineering. Also Business studies. Diana is not doing anything to jeopardise their hard work. Just because she has been selfish and fallen for someone else. So she will have to try to forget about Graham.

Graham still won't leave Diana alone, he's not going easily. But Diana keeps telling him no, "look Graham I've got some feelings for you too, but it's not going to happen because I love my husband and children too much to ever hurt them." Graham tells Diana, "I completely understand that and respect it so much. But just let me take you away to nice places, while I've got the money. Tony has to work away a lot, while he's away please spend it with me. I love you so much and will treat you right. I'm not asking you to run away with me. I understand you have been married for over 20 years, just let me be with you too. It can't do any harm if I know the score and am happy to share you. I just want to make you feel good and you are so beautiful you deserve to be treated like a princess. Which I am capable of doing, and would really enjoy making you feel good. Our love making will be amazing!"

Diana says Graham, "let me take you away one weekend while Tony is working away?" Diana thinking about it says, "Ok where are you going to take me then?" Graham happily says, "where ever you would love to go my darling." Then follows with, "I just want to be with you, it's not just about sex even though I love making love to you, more than I ever have in my life with anyone." Graham Diana says, "I love making love with you just as much, I get really excited just thinking about you." Graham says, "Do you feel like making love now? Because I do, we could go back to my place for a while. I'm feeling really horny just thinking about you. This is what you do to me." Diana exclaims, "me too Graham! I want you now."

Graham takes Diana by the hard, "if you've got nothing on now. Come with me and I'll drive back to my place?" Ok yes says Diana. So they go back to Graham's. Feeling like teenagers again. Ripping each other's clothes off quickly before they even get to his bedroom. Diana jumps on top of the bed giggling, "Come on Graham make mad passionate love to me." Graham slip's his hands between Diana's thighs and starts kissing her all over her body

Moaning she says, "I want you so much Graham!" He kisses her all the way down, then starts licking slowly at first, until Diana grabs his head closer and he starts licking faster until she's about to come. He stops quickly and says, "oh no not yet, I've not finished with you my love." She cries out, "don't tease me! I want you inside me now." He gladly obeys, but putting a condom on first, rubs himself up against her clit, Diana is moaning now oh Graham goodness I'm going to orgasm! So he quickly slips inside her pushing himself up against her slowly. Diana quickly switches positions and starts riding him so fast, he can't control himself and they both climax together. Graham quickly switches positions taking back control, he kisses her all over while pulling the vibrator out of the drawer, he pushes it up her bottom while going down on her. Diana is screaming so loudly now while he is getting really excited! Then Diana in complete control now. Puts the vibrator into Graham's bum while going down on him. It's Graham's turn to start moaning in ecstasy and shouting Diana's name out, "God I love you Diana, you're the best!" Before he ejaculates. Diana wanting more says, "Graham use the vibrator on me now for the last time, but it's not the last time. He brings Diana to orgasm more than she has ever orgasmed in her life! Diana lying there in complete bliss says, "Graham I have never orgasmed so much! I still feel tingly all over, I want you to feel the way I do." So she gets the vibrations all over his body while going down on him and then puts it up his bum until he is screaming out oh goodness I love you so fucking much! I don't want you to go home, stay the night with me." Luckily Tony won't be home tonight. Diana agrees and they carry on making love all night, until they are extremely exhausted. Graham whispers to Diana best fucking sex of my life. Before he drops off to sleep.

When Diana awakens still tingling all over her body. Waking Graham up says, "Are you ready to go again." Graham jumping up says, "Diana I'm always ready for you my love." So off they start again. Graham says, "Diana can I show you my sex toys? I know you'll love them." Diana replies, "Graham I would love to see them and try them out now hey." Both feeling excited get the sex toys out and start having a little play with them, there's some balls that you insert into you that stimulates the women's G spot. Just the slightest movement makes you feel like you're going to come. Well Graham putting one into Diana and going down on her. Makes her feel crazy and she just feels like she's going to orgasm, so she inserts one into Graham's bum and goes down on him too. They are in the 69 position and Graham shouts Diana I'm going to come. Diana says, "That's fine Graham just let it go." At the same time, Diana starts orgasming too. Then Graham putting on a condom as fast as he can, takes Diana from behind, Diana screaming out loud, as she's in another climax, feeling like she's in heaven. Wants Graham to be feeling the same way, so she finds the vibrator and slipping the ball out of his anal quickly places the vibrator up his bottom. While he's got Diana from behind, sends him crazy too. Both climaxing together and not wanting it to ever end. Graham thinking I need to move the position of the ball inside Diana to her bottom too. Diana loving it, switches her position, so she's in control and riding Graham. Starts slow then fast and faster until they're both screaming out loud and louder I'm coming. Having a rest, Diana turns to Graham. "You know when you came in my mouth I didn't mind the taste of you, the only other man I like the taste of their come is Tony. That's how I know you are meant for me like my husband." Graham replies, "Diana you have made my night so much, that meant a lot to me too, to let me ejaculate into your mouth, I love the taste of you so much, I can never get enough of you not ever. The more you give. The more I want. Don't know what it is about you Diana but you've totally got me, exactly where you want me. I'm yours, whenever you can get away with me, I'll take you wherever you want to go in the world my love. I mean that, don't worry how much it costs because money is nothing when it comes to you my love. With that Graham gently taking Diana onto his bed, and putting another condom on taking back control. Slowly pumping inside her says, "I love you so much Diana."

Chapter Nine

They are both extremely tired and just fall asleep cuddling each other.

When they awake, Graham asks Diana, "Where would you like to go my beautiful?" Diana replies, "I've always fancied Dubai." So Graham thinks Dubai it is then. Before they head to the travel agents, he makes love to her one last time. At the travel agents, feeling very giddy they book to go in January 2023.

Feeling excited about going Dubai, Diana turns to Graham and says, "Graham thank you for giving me something to look forward to. It's going to be amazing." And with that she rolls on top of him and slowly takes his pants off. Quickly she kisses him all around his stomach and his penis. Then taking the whole of his penis in her mouth starts licking and sucking until he comes in her mouth. Graham is in heaven, he loves her so much. He just wants to satisfy her all the time, so spreading her legs he kisses her all over taking her knickers off. He licks her all the way down until she is moaning and screaming I'm going to come. So he puts on a condom very quickly and lies on top of her and fucks her really hard until they both orgasm. Diana not wanting it to end sits on top of him and starts riding him until she is having multiple orgasms. Feeling satisfied she lies down and goes to sleep for a little while.

Waking up Diana watching Graham sleep thinks I'll just get the vibrator and place it on him and see what he does. Well he jumps up with the vibration on his penis and grabs Diana on his face, pleasuring her with his mouth all over her vagina until they both orgasm again, Diana's orgasms are so much more intense than Graham's, Diana just wishes he could orgasm as much as she does. But the thing is a women's orgasm are so much powerful than a man's. And thinking about that wonders why Men are more obsessed with sex than women. She thinks to herself. Somethings In life just don't make sense do they lol.

Graham turns to Diana and says, "I don't want you to go home tonight. What can I do to make you stay another night sexy?" She replies, "Just carry on what you're doing and I'll never want to go home." So Graham gets his sex toys out and says, "My love choose which one you want to try next?" She sees a massive vibrator and points to that one. He smiles and kisses her all over her body. Grabbing the huge vibrator, he slips it in between her legs and pushing it inside her vagina, starts pushing it really hard until she's screaming out I'm coming. Well Graham I have had the best time with you ever, but it's back to work life tomorrow for us both. All good things have to come to an end eventually sadly.

Chapter Ten

Back in work, they both are deep in their thoughts, remembering the great weekend they've just had and all their love making. They both are feeling horny just thinking about it, Diana pictures Graham in her mind all the sexy things he was doing to her, and because it's so quiet in work. She spreads her legs out across her chair and putting her hands down her knickers, starts rubbing her clit and sliding a finger inside herself too, getting really excited wishing Graham was there. In the meantime Graham is buying some beautiful flowers for Diana, thinking I'll go and take them to her to cheer her up on her first day back, and of course for Valentine's Day. Walking in on her. Says, "I can see you're busy working." Diana nearly dies of embarrassment. Graham starts laughing and says, "Let me help you" putting on a condom and bending Diana over the table fucks her from behind, it doesn't take Diana long to orgasm! She says, "I'm so embarrassed Graham, you wasn't supposed to see me doing that!" Graham laughing saying, "Don't worry my love. That has just turned me on so much. Do you mind if I play with myself?" Before he can do anything, Diana is on her knees unzipping his pants and puts his penis into her mouth, sucking until he comes in her mouth. "Thank you Graham for my beautiful flowers, this has been my best first day back ever. I love you." Graham says, "I love you so much too beautiful."

Diana feeling so horny. She just wants Graham right now. So rings him up and says, "Graham I am so fucking horny. I just want you right now to fuck me hard and harder until I orgasm." Graham running out into his car, jumps in and driving to Diana at full speed. Runs into her and grabbing her roughly says, "Is this what you want my sexy, horny and beautiful bitch? I've missed you so much, and was so excited when you rang me and said you wanted me inside you." He gets on his knees and pulling her to his mouth, starts rubbing his tongue up and down her clit slowly until she starts moaning. Graham go faster. I'm so excited! He obliges quickly until she's screaming I'm going to come. He stops and putting a condom on, grabs her on top of him and fucking her really hard. They orgasm together.

Now focusing on work, Diana sits at her desk, back to completely putting her mind into work mode. She is back on form. Second Day of back at work, Tuesday 15th February 2022. She has had her fun with Graham and boy was it fun. She even missed her anniversary with Tony of 20 years marriage, because he was working away. But enjoyed the weekend before Valentine's Day with Graham. He took her out to wine, dine and 69 her which they had both enjoyed immensely. Diana had never been this sexual and adventurous as now. Which she blames on the menopause. Little does Graham know, he thinks she is in her early 40's like him, Well he just presumed she was the same age as him 40, if he only knew she was 9 years older than himself (49). Diana was blessed with very good young looking skin that she inherited from her mum. There was a lot Graham didn't know about Diana. For instance he didn't know she had multiple sclerosis. Because she was on a very good MS treatment. So looked like there was nothing wrong with her. And she felt fit too, if only he knew her 10 years ago, when she was in a wheelchair and couldn't walk. To be fair that was nothing to do with her having M.S. To cut a long story short. I'll have to continue on a new paragraph....

Well Diana was unlucky to have a very arrogant consultant Dr Dick, who she hated with a passion. He preached that every patient should learn about their own M.S, and when they did. He doesn't listen to them. Because he thinks he knows best.

He was very hard work. This is probably the reason why Tony's suffering with Depression now in 2022. And doesn't know what's wrong with himself. Keeps saying over and over again. I have no purpose, but Diana reminds him that she loves him. And that she and the kids (including Leo) are his purpose. She can't drum it into him enough, she keeps telling him also that he's been through so much with herself. Having Chronic Fatigue. Worst time of both their lives. You see, this horrible condition. Also known as M.E, doesn't just affect the sufferer. But also the family of the suffering. Diana recalls a conversation she once had with a beautician. A few years ago at Center Parcs but can't remember her name, as she would love to apologise to her big time! The conversation went...beautician says, what's wrong with you? As Diana was in a wheelchair but could also get out and walk a little bit. Diana explains saying, "I have M.S. So can walk for a little while, but get tired quickly. So then need to get in my wheelchair." Beautician says, "I have M.E it's very similar to M.S isn't it?" Diana says, "Not sure all I know is with M.S, it shows up on a brain scan." Insinuating that M.S is a lot worse than M.E. But now with suffering from them both, knows this is not the case. Now knowing M.E is worse than M.S. May be the reason why Diana had to learn the hard way. And boy has she learnt. And would just love to apologise to this beautician so much for her ignorant comment. So if you're reading this and can remember the conversation. Just know how sorry I am from the heart. Also writing this book has helped me see the truth. It was Diana's own fault after all. Diana is a true believer in karma. And believes this is her own karma. But at the same time shouldn't be affecting Tony her Amazing husband. He really doesn't deserve what he has been through. Anyway, Diana used to be in tears arguing with Dr Dick in his office, because he wouldn't listen to her. She even said once, because she was that angry at him! In front of her M.S nurse (who she thought was her friend. To her and Tony) but her M.S nurse Francine took Diana outside to calm her down, and discourage her to not get rid of Dr Dick, because if she went to Dr Tala she would find him even worse saying, "Dr Tala wouldn't speak up because he's not as confident as Dr Dick, and that Diana wouldn't be able to cope with him, she would be pulling her hair out!". But now Diana has Dr Tala she loves him. Diana thinks Dr Tala is the second best consultant she's ever had, after her most favourite Dr Mox but unfortunately he moved to Sweden. And Diana lost the best Consultant she had ever known. Fortunately she now has Dr Tala and is doing so well with him. Makes her think, "if only she hadn't took Francine's advice!" But to be honest. And this is giving Dr Dick the benefit of the doubt, even though she doesn't want to, because he's the worst and most arrogant Consultant she's ever had the misfortune of meeting. I'll tell you what happened, so you can judge for yourself.

I'll start from the beginning. Diana was on a drug to help slow down her M.S, called Gilenya. She was the 5th person in the country to start on it, even though it came with some very bad side effects. Like death, skin cancer and could affect your kidneys and liver. Which you had to have regular blood tests every 3 months, which didn't bother Diana. Needles never affected her. But what did scare Diana was the death penalty. And Skin Cancer. But there was no mention of chronic fatigue. Which when you are actually bed bound with it for 5 years, is the worst side effect of all. Diana recalls her husband making a remark, when they were in hospital to take the first tablet. He said, "This is a leap of faith!" The thing is, the first dose of Gilenya had to be taken in hospital only. Diana remembered when she first got this drug, feeling like she had won the lottery. Wow how life can trick you, then how life can help you out too, so always stay humble and thankful. We just don't know what is around the corner. Happiness or sadness. Well I hope Diana and her family have lots of happiness from this day on.

Back to my story. Diana worked hard to stay fit, like going to the gym, doing a Pilates class, which she absolutely loved, and going swimming while her children were in school. She thought and still thinks today, this is the best way to live your life. But Dr Dick (who was very over weight and couldn't even walk down the corridor without getting out of breath) kept telling Diana to bring the reigns in. But she only did what she felt ok doing. She also went on plenty of walks. And loved her life. But then Diana started feeling more fatigued. She listened to her body and rested when needed to. Anyway the fatigue became a lot worse. As she had to keep going for brain scans. Until she was completely bed bound. Still Dr Dick, had no solution, except Diana and Tony suspected it was the Gilenya, but unfortunately there was no new drug to switch to. Anyway 5 years of torture for Diana and her family. Tony had to still work, as well as look after his family as best as he could. Kids suffered, had to stop their activities. Gabrielle was a very good swimmer and swam for Aqua Seals competitive swimming, but only could carry on because Tony used to take her when he could, plus Grandma and her Auntie Joanne would help take her too. Cameron loved sprinting and was very fast, he also went to a competitive running club, which he absolutely loved, because he was on top form and used to be one of the best runners in Rochdale and competed too, Grandma had to take him because Tony was working he had his second knee dislocation in year seven. Cameron had to give up running, probably was best for Cameron. Because he has very bad knees which he inherited from his mum. He had his first knee dislocation at the age of 10. He was just in the conservatory closing the blinds, when Diana heard him scream, but she couldn't do anything, only shout Tony, he ran down the stairs, and when he seen Cameron's knee hanging out the side, he shouted to Diana he's broken his knee, and picked him up, when Diana seen Cameron's knee on the other side of his leg, she just burst out crying. Tony rang an ambulance, and they took about two hours to arrive, because Cameron could still breathe, he wasn't classed as an emergency. Which was an absolute joke. When the paramedics arrived, Diana lay there feeling so hopeless and guilty because she was told it was her fault, but when the paramedic finally arrived. Diana was fed up with him for taking so long, also because she felt so helpless and snapped at the paramedic saying, "Can you just give him some pain relief before you start trying to help him move, he's been lay there for hours with his knee on the other side of his leg. The extremely nice and caring man, seems to understand Diana's frustration and says, "I am so sorry Cameron has had to wait so long, but unfortunately he is not classed as an emergency." Diana snapped saying, "You know what the stupid woman said who answered the phone, she said just give him two Paracetamol, what the hell is that going to do for him, It's a flaming joke! So I gave him 2 Ibuprofen and 2 paracetamol, because you was talking so long." The lovely paramedic said, "I really do understand, but had to go out to the more severe, who were struggling to breathe." Diana started to calm down a lot and says, "I am so sorry too, but when you're just lay here and can't do anything to help your son, it's the worst feeling in the world!" He gives Cameron some Morphine after doing all the checks on him and asking lots of questions, to make sure it's safe to give to him, when the Morphine kicks in, Cameron doesn't stop talking. Diana is so happy he's out of pain, then the paramedic puts his knee back into place, he then has to take him hospital with Tony for X-Rays to make sure his knee is back in place properly.

Poor Cameron had to go and see a Consultant who specialised in knees, and he said, "He has the worst knees he's ever seen, especially his left one, which he hardly has any groove to keep it in place. So is waiting for an operation on them both. Cameron is due to have his first surgery on his left knee in July 2022. His right knee is still very bad, but has a little bit more groove holding it in place, than his left knee. The recovery period is estimated at one year, then he can have his second surgery on his right knee. Cameron can't wait to be able to walk without worrying about them dislocating.

Because Diana is suffering with Chronic Fatigue, she can only have one carer coming into help her called Shirley. She is brilliant with Diana and really understands her condition, which not a lot of people do. Even Doctors struggle to understand this very complex condition. Which Diana struggles with mostly. Luckily Tony knew of a colleague, who specialised in chronic fatigue and could help Diana start to learn how to deal with this devastating condition! It was not a quick fix. But it gave Diana hope, and she did exactly what Dr

Calm told her to do. It was very frustrating to try to improve from this condition, as it was such a repetitive process, push it too fast and you would crash and have to go back to the beginning. Diana was a very determined woman and nether gave up. When she had her heart set on something, would fight to the end. After a long time, Tony heard of a new treatment becoming available. So spoke with Diana about this great news. But like everything in new treatments for M.S, You have to apply for funding first. A very long story cut short, Diana was accepted for this new drug, or should I say infusion called Ocrevus.

Chapter Eleven

Diana got rid of Dr Dick, and was starting to feel a bit happy again. Until she had a massive relapse! Worse one she had ever had. Unfortunately when Diana came off her drug Gilenya, she had to wait 4 weeks until she could start her new treatment, also when you came off this drug, there was a risk of a massive relapse. Which is exactly what happened to Diana, she didn't know where she was. Could not talk, eat food, had to be fed through a tube through her nose. Doctors also wanted to put a peg in Diana's stomach. But Gabrielle said to her dad, "No don't let them do that to my mum." Tony agreed, told doctors no. Diana could not move her legs or arms. Especially on her right hand side, her more prominent side as well. Couldn't open her right hand at all, her fingers are fused closed tight. The attack happened in 2019, and in 2022 she was still struggling. Spent 9months in hospital, where her sister Kelsey would come and visit her a lot, you see Diana didn't see Kelsey a lot, but when Diana was in a bad way, she was always there for her. Then 3months in The Floyd Unit, which is a Rehab hospital, where you go to recover. Before she went into Rehab, she had such a lovely carer called Susan, who Diana absolutely thought the World of, but unfortunately when she came back home....Susan was gone, she had been sacked because of a total misunderstanding, her boss said she missed a call and fired her, so when Diana came home from the Rehab Centre, Susan was gone. Diana was so gutted and was really sad for a long time, because she just had all different carers coming in, some didn't have a clue what they were doing and was just thrown into the deep end. In the

Floyd Unit Diana had to learn to be able to sit up in a wheelchair. Physios never thought she would be able to bend her legs again. But the determination of Diana proved everyone wrong. Physios told Diana she defied science and they wanted her to run her own clinic, In the NHS. Diana is really considering this. Because if she can help people never give up. And realise they can do anything they put their minds to, then she would feel better, that she has helped someone to recover. She has to have Carers coming in every day. Four times a day, her main Carer's consists of Ellie, who is her favourite carer because if it wasn't for Ellie and her husband. Diana wouldn't be able to stand up has she does now. Because Diana had to wait a while for physios to come out. When she got out of the Floyd Unit. She has always said it was down to her Amazing carer Ellie, and hubby. Hannah has took over Ellie, because Ellie has had to go into the office. Mainly because of her back problems, Ellie is only 21 but because she started working as a carer from a young age. She already suffers from a very bad back at such a young age. Life has not been kind to Ellie, and to be honest she really doesn't deserve it, because she is such a beautiful and lovely young woman, Hannah who is Ellie's best friend, and has learnt from the best. She is so funny too when she is trying to dance. Diana is so determined to walk again, especially so she can show Hannah and Ellie how to dance lol. Ellie and Hannah rent a place together, so it's probably best they don't work together anymore. Because they would be doing each other's heads in spending so much time together, Pam (Pam is Diana's inspiration, she is coming up to sixty, and is training to do an half marathon (13 miles) Diana is so in awe of her.) Kelsey Who has learned everything she knows from Hannah and is becoming a very good carer and person. Diana really likes and appreciates her, Charlee Who really believes in Diana and is giving Diana the confidence to write this book. She is so funny. Diana doesn't see Charlee as much as she'd love to, but when they get together, they have a good chat and laugh so much with her tales of things that happen to her. Such as when she went into a man client, he said to her, "I've got some money over there, would you like to get in bed with me and I'll pay you?" Charlee was absolutely mortified! But when she told Diana. They had to laugh about it. Fair to say she won't be going back to him ever again. Breanna Diana loves her too, she is such a character, very beautiful and a very good inspirational speaker. If Diana had half her confidence, she would be very happy, Katie Bowater, she is good fun, a very good dancer like Diana used to be, An Amazing cake decorator just like Diana used to be as well. But because Diana's fingers are fused together on her right hand, sadly her cake making days are over. But her daughter Gabrielle who is 19, has learnt so much from her Mum. So will help her to bake and decorate the cakes, my main newest carers are, Sundas, who is a very good person and carer, very good at blow drying Diana's hair, Diana would be lost without her, Lydia a great carer and good laugh. She also drives, which the Care company needs more of to be honest. Because all the nondrivers have to rely on taxis, which are not the best to be fair! Dawn who was once banned! But now looking back can see it was a total miss understanding on both sides. So Diana is so glad she's giving her a second chance because she loves her, she's so funny and caring and is definitely becoming one of Diana's favourite carers, she also drives, Emily she's a crazy girl, but such good fun, Diana can really have a laugh with her. And believe me when you are suffering, is one of the most important things, Stacey Diana has not known her long, but really likes her, she is very caring and knows her stuff, like music and films. Which are Diana's favourite at the moment, she would be lost without her entertainment, and last of all Georgia, Diana has only met her a few times, but can tell she's a lovely person and gets a very good vibe from her. Which Diana always believes her senses so much. Georgia has also got a 3 year old toddler. And is related to Garry Oldie, crazy thing is, Diana knows Garry as he is married to her friend Andrea, who used to be Diana's best friend growing up. Don't really know some of the other new carers enough to comment on, but what she knows so far. Is that Diana really likes Stacey, Zoe, Jessica, Georgia and Dawn are the newest. But overall Diana has a really good team looking after her, and would be lost without them. So a Massive Thank you to them all from the bottom of my heart.

I'll tell you the story of Bouncer and why Diana had a baseball bat. One day Diana was just taking Bouncer on his usual walk until she sees another girl with 3 dogs, 1 boxer and 2 Alsatians which she couldn't handle. The boxer gets away from her and runs at Bouncer and goes straight for his neck, (Well Boxers jaws lock when they get their teeth into something) Unfortunately it was poor Bouncer's throat, he was so scared he pooed in the middle of the road! I was also so scared and I screamed at the stupid girl to get her dog off my dog, but she couldn't control the dog. But luckily a man ran over and got the boxer off Bouncer. Thank goodness for that man. He saved Bouncer that day. But I was so angry at that stupid girl! The Amazing man told me to get home with Bouncer, but I was too angry at the girl, I was shouting loudly to her where did she live, so she writes down her address and gives it to the man to give it to me. Then I took Bouncer home and when I saw the state of his neck. I rang the police, who told me there was nothing they could do about dog's behaviour. So Diana was fuming and said, "This girl shouldn't have been out with 3 dogs that she couldn't handle. What if it had been a kid! I've got the address of this girl and she needs a warning! Before someone gets badly hurt! Anyway the police go around to her house, but obviously SHE's given me the WRONG address. So I took Bouncer to the vets and they treated the massive lumps he had on his neck. But I never wanted to feel that helpless again. So I got a baseball bat and took it with me, every time I took Bouncer out. The funny thing is that GUY who SAVED Bouncer, was roughly the same age as the GUY Who saved me when I was being bullied in High school! Diana thinks IT'S VERY STRANGE!

Diana's doing so well in her physio, with Ann, Tammy and Rebecca. She can now transfer from bed to wheelchair, and vice versa. Doesn't need her hoist anymore. Which made her life so much better. The next step is to walk again. She's always believed she can do this, so won't give up! The key to recovery is 3 things Belief, faith and hope. If you've got these, then there's no stopping you. You can do anything you put your mind to. Believe in yourself. Diana is living proof of this. Diana is very lucky to have a beautiful family, who always support her. This is also a major part of the recovery. Also learn how to meditate the proper way. This can be so helpful.

Scientists still haven't found a cure for M.S, but never lose hope because they are amazing and very, very clever. Diana is due to go to hospital in a month's time for her infusion, and while she's there is going to be asking some questions about a theory she has!?! A long time ago, when she was in her late 20's, about 27 to be more precise. She had the misfortune of meeting her boyfriend Jim, a bouncer who seemed really nice and genuine, in sunny Blackpool. But little did she know he was going to be her undoing! At the time she had a major crush on Nicolas Cage, and when she met Jim, she thought he looked so much like him. So fell for him instantly. Anyway while she was with him, he took her to get her first dog. Diana had fell in love with Golden Labradors at first sight. When she first seen them as an 8 year old. Remember the Andrex puppies? Well from that moment she was in love with them. And begged her mum for one, but her mum was too house proud to let Diana have one, instead she bought her a cuddly toy Labrador dog, who Diana absolutely adored, and loved so much as if it was real. So the only thing good about meeting Jim was that he took her to buy a proper one. Diana bonded straight away with her dog. Who she named Bouncer, because he bounced everywhere in the house. She loved him so much. The funny thing is Bouncer would only go to Diana. They say animals can sense the truth about people. As much As they fake it. A person cannot fool a dog. He may have fooled Diana at first, but no, not Bouncer.

Anyway Diana was happy for a long time, only because of Bouncer, Jim would make her cringe every time they had sex. Diana started to save her hard earned money to eventually be able to get away from the false Jim. She worked in a petrol station, and hated leaving Bouncer every day. But had to work to get money. Diana shamingly had 2 abortions while with Jim. Because Diana would never go on the pill, but knew deep down that she was never going to stay with him. Aborted her babies, which she punished herself for a long time.

But once she met the real deal Tony her husband, she then knew the reason she aborted her 2 babies. So the only advice I can give to girls. Who are in the same predicament as Diana, is no matter how much pressure you are getting from the professionals, to keep the baby that's growing inside of you. Always listen to your inner voice, and what it's telling you. Because only you know best! I wish someone had given me this advice, when I needed it the most.

Eventually Diana made the right choice to leave Jim. And never looked back. But only looking back now, to figure out the reason why she has M.S, anyway before she finally left this poor excuse for a man. Diana had never been so stressed out in her whole life! And when she told Jim she was leaving him. He acted like a baby. Running to his mum to tell her. But Diana was having none of his rubbish. So he thought he could do and say anything to Diana! Like, "some girls are going to beat you up." Diana scoffed! "Whatever" Trying to keep as calm as she could. But then Jim calls her a slag and spits in her face. Diana snaps like she has never snapped before and grabs the baseball bat. Diana only had a baseball bat in the first place to protect Bouncer from other viscous dogs, which is another story. Hits him once on the head, then twice and eventually going to hit him a third time, until she hears a voice in her head. Telling her not to do it. So she drops the bat and listens. Thank God she did, because Jim went to the hospital with a fractured skull. And the doctor told him, "one more hit on the head and he would have been dead!" But before you all go feeling sorry for him, carry on reading before you pass judgment.

Anyway one day Diana came home from work, to find Bouncer lying on the floor, not able to move. Not touched his food! Well if you knew Bouncer, you'd know there had to be something seriously wrong with him. Not to eat his food. Crying Diana took bouncer to the vets. Vet told her, "He must have fell down the stairs, because he has broken his back!" Diana in shock and sobbing even more, says, "How could he have fallen down the stairs." Vet thinking, "he must have missed a step and then just tumbled down." Diana not thinking straight, takes him home, and takes time off work to look after him the best way she can. And just be with him as much she could.

If only she knew at the time that Jim had kicked him down the stairs! In a way it was a good job, she didn't because she would have been in prison, serving time for murder! See how sometimes life can help you out. So because Diana was so stressed out. Even her Auntie Mo said, "She had never seen Diana like this in her life." She woke up one day covered from head to toe in red spots. So Diana in panic goes to her doctors. Walking into the surgery, office staff taking one look at her. Takes her into another room. And brings the doctor to her. Doctor examines Diana and feeling her glands says, "You have Infectious Mononucleosis, also known as Glandular Fever." He tells her, "You will feel better in a few weeks, and when you get down to your last spot. You are no longer contagious. That's when you can go back to work. In the meantime stay at home and have plenty of rest, and drink lots of water." Doctor also says, "You don't ever get over Glandular fever you know." Diana not quite knowing what to make of this, and still doesn't understand that statement today. But thinks he must have meant it stays in your system for life, and thinking, wondering if that's one of the reasons she has M.S. She goes for her Infusion in a few weeks and thinks I'll ask my Consultant.

Chapter Twelve

Looking back on her life, Jim wasn't the first waist of space boyfriend she had been out with. Oh no! There was Darren, Darren was unique, she had never met anyone like him. And never has since thank Goodness. Diana was living in Ashton-in-Maker field, and working in a Petrol Station. Diana was extremely popular, and most people just went in to see her. This very handsome half-cast man walked in dressed in his firemen uniform, and got talking to her. After a while this confident fireman asked Diana out on a date, Diana happily said yes. So went out on a few dates, before she started getting threatening phone calls. From a girl, who was accusing her of stealing her boyfriend. Diana had enough of this girl and said, "Come down and threaten me to my face." So this girl called Kelly walking through the door with a baby in a pram says, "I've been seeing Darren for a while now, and you're seeing him behind my back." Diana in shock says, "I had no idea he was seeing anyone else." So when Darren came in to see her when he finished work. Diana wasn't very happy and said, "I didn't know you was seeing another girl called Kelly!" Darren looking a bit nervous said, "I finished with Kelly, when I met you honestly." So Diana falling for it because she liked him so much, told him about the threatening phone calls and how Kelly had come in and told her she had been seeing you for a while now, well he just laughed saying, "I was seeing her until I met you. Then I finished with her because I fell for you." Diana flattered decided to give him the benefit of the doubt. The next chapter is all about Darren.

Chapter Thirteen

I have to tell you all about Darren, just in case you ever meet anyone like him. Well it just got worse from here. He told Diana that he was a football player. He looked like a famous footballer. When they were out together, men would come over and ask him was he such a body? Well football never meant anything to Diana. But Darren would act like he was him. Then he said to Diana, "I have to tell you something. He told her he used to be a footballer, but not anymore because of an injury." Diana didn't know what to say but, "I'm sorry you lost your career because of an injury." But she wasn't convinced, so looked him up. The article said he was still playing, and I must admit he did look like him. But Diana could tell it wasn't him. So she pulled Darren up about it. All he could do was laugh and say, "I was just having a laugh."

Well the lies just got worse. Even him being a fireman was a load of rubbish. He told Kelly he was a paramedic, until she found out the truth about him. Well that's a very long story, and actually Diana and Kelly became good friends from it. Even best friends eventually. They lived next door to each other in Rochdale, and then together in a house in Blackpool. So you just don't know where life is going to take you.

They ended up in Rochdale from Ashton first, because Diana lost her house she was renting. So she moved to Rochdale to live with her sister jasmine, then Kelly wanted to come and live in Rochdale too. So they rented two flats next door to each other on a council estate. These flats were in such a bad area in Rochdale but they were all they could get with dogs. Diana had Bouncer and Kelly had Tiger an Alsatian

Diana had very high standards. So her Auntie Mo painted it for her. And Diana made it extremely clean, put nice furniture in and carpets. Bought a modem T.V and hi-fi, it looked a lot better than Kelly's. Then they got in with some Asian wannabe gangsters. Big mistake! Diana and Kelly weren't racist. And thought they were ok. A few of them were, one of them really fancied Diana. He was really nice, so Diana went out with him for a little while, then there was Achy who seemed ok at first. Who really fancied Diana, Diana wasn't interested at first, but he wouldn't give up. Then he wormed his way in and Diana started to like him. They started to go out and Diana started to fall for him. He was a proper charmer. At first he treated Diana really well, but when he knew he had her. Started to show his true colours

Achy was married and lived in a very respectful place. But was bored with his wife, so when he saw Diana, he wanted her straight away. He was so charming and won her over. Diana really started to like him a lot. Achy met her Auntie Mo and she really liked him too. Diana ended up sleeping with Achy because she thought he was for real. Stupid really because he was married. But girls always seem to fall for the bad boys. Anyway situations like this always end badly.

Kelly got in a bad situation with some lad she was dating and his friends. Thought they were gangsters. But because she pushed them too far, they wanted to kill her. They all liked Diana, so was still ok with her. Anyway when things got too hot to handle for Kelly, she ran back to Ashton leaving Diana behind. But Diana had really started like living in her flat with Bouncer so stayed there. But after a few months things took a turn for the worst. The lads that were looking for Kelly started to get really mad because she owed them money. Thinking Diana was hiding her in her flat, they threatened, that they were going to throw fireworks through the letter box. So Diana rang the police. They were a total waste of time. Diana waiting over two hours for them to arrive. Rang the police back, and was told they had already been out. Looked around the back. Saw no one was there and went away. Diana fuming! Said, "For a start, they were around the front threatening to post fireworks through my letter box. With just me and my dog in the flat, and no way of getting out the back.

So Diana angrily gets a knife and goes out with Bouncer. And guess what! Two security guards approach her, and say, "What you doing with that knife." Diana glaring at them like if looks could kill! Says, "Protecting me and my dog, because no one else will. And where on earth were you two, when all of them lads were here. Threatening to put fireworks through my door? All they could say is, "drop that knife, before someone gets hurt." So Diana tells them to fuck off. They ring the police and the police tells Diana, "to calm down or they will have to arrest her." Laughing Diana says, "Couldn't care flaming less, so do one!" Police arrest Diana, she puts up a good fight, but can't do much once in hand cuffs. All Diana cares about is what's going to happen to Bouncer. So one police woman says, "Do you have any family living around here?" Diana tells her about Jasmine and Derick who live not far from here in Milnrow. She rings them and Derick comes to the police station, to take Diana and Bouncer home to his house.

So Diana stayed there for a little while, until she seen a nice flat. Near where she used to live. That took animals. So she enquired. Luckily (or unluckily) it was very affordable. Diana was very grateful to her big sister Jasmine. But didn't really like living there, because when Derick was drunk. He used to try it on with her. Diana didn't want to tell jasmine and upset her. So Diana just worked, took Bouncer on long walks, and tried to stay away from Derick as much as she could when he had a drink. It was such a shame because Derick was really nice and helpful. When sober, but he spoiled himself when drunk. Anyway Diana was very independent, and just needed to make her own way in life.

Chapter Fourteen

So Diana moved into her new flat with Bouncer. Made it really homely. Her Auntie Mo used to come and visit a lot. Diana was still seeing Achy and went out quite a bit, on her days off. Diana got another job in a different petrol station. Things were going okay, until she couldn't just walk down the street, without being hassled by Asian men asking her out on a date. They were so cheeky and she started to hate them. She told Achy about it. He just said, "What do you want me to do about it!" I suppose he was right. There was not a lot he could do. But things went from bad to worse with Achy. She went out with him in his car to visit some girls. That he thought Diana would get on with. But oh no! They were so jealous of her beauty. One girl was staring at her and started a fight. So Diana sticking up for herself, fought back. Until this other girl, picking up a bottle, was about to smash it over Diana's head! But Achy grabs the bottle off her and quickly getting Diana out of there. But Diana was still angry. And tried to get out of the car while it was still moving. Achy had to slam on the brakes. Grabs Diana before she could jump out of the car. It was probably the most decent thing Achy had ever done for Diana that night Diana thought to herself. But then spoils it, when he kicked her off outside her flat and drives off. Leaving her there on the floor. In the freezing cold and drunk. Luckily a couple who lived nearby, had seen it all, and picked Diana up and got her into her flat safely. But they were so disgusted with what they seen, they reported it to the head of the Asian Community who lived nearby. But Diana didn't even know existed. She was very thankful to the couple that lived nearby.

Diana waking up with a massive hangover, and so embarrassed to walk out the flat. Thought to herself, "Wow! How I've let myself go. And said to herself, I definitely need to finish with Achy." So that is what she does. And surprisingly, she gets burgled, while at work. Diana walking down the street, sees Bouncer sat outside the door. Seeing her he happily runs to her with his tail wagging so fast. Diana so surprised, but happily hugs Bouncer to death. But thinking this is the last straw! I can't stay here anymore. I have to move right now. I'm Done! I've finally had enough! So telling her landlord she wants to move out, he is so gutted. And begs her to stay saying, "I'll have a word with the Asian Community leader. He'll sort them out." But no, when Diana's mind was set there was no budging it. She apologised but said, "No I'm sorry I can't stay here now especially because I could have lost Bouncer." The landlord just wanted her to stay because she was the best payer he'd ever had, and so clean.

Diana knew it was Achy, there's only Achy that wouldn't take Bouncer, because he knew how much he meant to her. She didn't care about all the other stuff that had gone. It was just stuff that you could replace. Anyway Diana rang Kelly, told her what happened, and Kelly said, "Do you fancy moving back to Blackpool?" Diana immediately said yes and with that they were gone. Diana said, "I'm not going back to South Shore, but will definitely try North Shore out." So that's where they went, it was great for a long time. They partied every night. Their nicknames the bouncers gave them was, 'Heaven and Hell', went shopping nearly every day. Diana had a figure to die for. So acting out because of everything she'd been through. Kelly would write cheques out to pay for their clothes, from Diana's cheque book. Then Diana would report it stolen. Diana felt like Julia Roberts from Pretty women.

Because she had such an amazing body and face to go with it. Diana loved her clothes so much and everything fit her perfectly.

Diana was spoilt for choice, and just wanted to buy everything. Diana hated banks with a passion! Especially TSB. Because TSB was the worst out of them all. They made Nellie, Diana's mum's life a living hell! And Diana could never ever forgive them for that. Nellie brought three children up on her own. Very well, living of Social benefits because she couldn't work. This reminds me of the song/rap from Two Pack, Dear mama. Nellie was suffering from Depression/Anxiety very badly. Doctor put her on antidepressants called Activan which only made her feel worse. In fact when Nellie died. There was a court case going on for people who were on Activan. They were all going to get compensation, for long tem use. No-one should have been on them for over 2 years. Nether mind for over 25 years, like Nellie! She would have got a very good pay out in Court, if still alive. But no. They found out too late.

Chapter Fifteen

Diana had to ring the courthouse, to let them know that her mum had passed away. They told her, she could get the compensation for her Mum. But Diana didn't feel right receiving the money, for something she didn't suffer. And anyway she knew if something seems too good to be true, it usually is.

Story of Nellie's life, she never ever got what she deserved in Life. Just all the bad stuff. Just wasn't fair. If you all knew Nellie, like everyone did, you would know, to know her was to love her. She was definitely special. One of Heaven's fallen Angels. Nellie prayed every night before she went to sleep. She always said you didn't have to go to Church to Believe in God or pray. She prayed for everyone in the World to be safe, and not be ill or hungry. One thing she never prayed for, was money. As much as they needed it. She would say, "Don't ever pray for money or material things. Just people, children and animals." Diana's mum was perfect. Except she liked to go out to drink and dance. She absolutely loved music, but had to drink to dance. She never had any confidence to just go out and party. Which was such a shame. She was an angel in the shape of her Mum. Which is from a song, Ed Sheeran sings.

If only Nellie could see herself, like everyone else did. She would know she was perfect, and could do anything she wanted in life. It was one of her traits that she passed down to Diana unfortunately. She was so tough and could beat anybody up, but didn't believe in violence. Only when she seen someone being bullied. Then she would go into a rage!

Watch out. She turned into the Incredible Hulk! She passed down to all of her children. Especially Jasmine, who could fight just like her mum, then it was Kelsey. She was only small, but extremely strong. She used to be a body builder. And one of the best in Middleton. There was an article in the newspaper about Kelsey, and how good her body building was. And Diana got her mum's Strength emotionally. And physically, (but only when pushed too far, then she would snap like she could take anyone on and kill them.)

Diana has always been so angry about what happened to her mum. But more angry about how people took advantage of Nellie's generosity. Even Jasmine her eldest, (took so much advantage of her mum.) Took Diana a very long time to forgive her eldest sister. But when she finally did. They got back to where they were. They had always been the closest to each other. Jasmine proved to Diana, that she was always there for her, countless times in her life.

This was one of the times that Jasmine was a God send to Diana, Diana was told that her lease was up and she had to move out. Dave who she was living with was lucky enough to be able to go back home. But Diana didn't want to have to move away from Ashton in Maker-field, she had built a good life there. Diana tried her best to look for something she could afford. But could only find accommodation to share with complete strangers. Anyway because she was desperate. Was willing to do. Diana went to visit these places, but wasn't having a lot of luck, until one became available to share with two lads who she didn't know.

When jasmine found out, she said to come to Milnrow and live with them. Diana was very grateful but at the same time was gutted! She had to leave Ashton. But then thought afterwards, "I could live with Jasmine and still travel to Ashton in Maker-field to work." So that is what she did. Diana had to be up every morning at 4am to get ready for work. She left the house at 6.15am to be in work for 7am to open the petrol station up. Diana took turns with Dave to open up the patrol station. At the time it was very awkward to have to work with Dave. As Diana had fell out with him.

Chapter Sixteen

Anyway Graham gets in touch with Diana at work. They'd not been in touch for a while, and Graham had missed Diana loads, Diana had also missed Graham a lot. And the sex was Amazing! Both had missed that so much. So Graham picks Diana up and takes her back to his house. Graham shows Diana how much he has missed her, by picking her up and taking her to his bed. He lies her down and undressing her he says, "What have you missed the most beautiful?" She replies, "I've missed the sex toys the most." So he pulls out the balls and inserts it inside her vagina. While Diana taking Graham's pants down inserts one into his bum. Both getting excited. Diana kisses Graham all over his body until she gets to his penis, then starts sucking until Graham is moaning so loud! He says, "Baby I'm going to come."

Graham rolls Diana onto her front and fucks her up the arse, until Diana is moaning loud and louder. She starts screaming, "Graham you're the best! I've missed this so much. I'm going to come." So both of them climaxing and feeling like they're in heaven. Diana wanting more sits on Graham's face, he's loving it. He licks her clit slowly and softly. Until Diana grabs his head and pulls it into her more, so he starts licking faster and harder until Diana's screaming I'm coming.

Graham inserts his finger inside Diana to take the ball out and places a condom on. He makes love to Diana so passionately, saying how much he loves her. Diana says, "Graham I love you so much too, I just don't want you to never stop making love to me ever." Graham starts pushing harder and harder until both orgasm together. Both lying in bliss, look at each other and say we've missed this so much.

Diana pulling the ball out of his bum inserts the massive vibrator up his bum, until he shouts oh wow! Push it harder and faster. Graham giving out a massive scream at once comes so loudly! It seems to last forever and ever again he shouts!! Again please that was the best orgasm I've ever had, so pulling Diana onto his face licks so hard and quickly until Diana is moaning and screaming I'm coming! Putting a condom on, grabs Diana and pulls her on top of him. Shouting ride me baby ride me, so Diana obliges him and rides Graham fast and faster until they both orgasm together again. Diana still wanting more, grabs the massive vibrator and turns it on, putting the vibrations on to her clit also pulls Graham on to her, so Graham can feel the vibrations on his dick too. They are both moaning so loud and louder! Until both climax together. Both lying there in complete bliss, Graham says, "when am I taking you to Dubai my beautiful?"

Diana turns to Graham and says, "I would love to go with you as soon as I can get away from it all. "I'll check with work as to when I can take my next holiday break." That is the first thing she does, when back in work the following day. Diana rings Graham up and says, "I can get two weeks off at the end of the month." Graham feeling really excited rushing to the travel agents. Books 2 weeks away at the end of the month. Rings Diana telling her, "We are both booked to go my beautiful."

Chapter Seventeen

Diana finished work and tells Tony, "I am going away with the girls at the end of the month love." He nods his head yes and then he kisses her all over her body and tells her, "I have missed you so much. All I want to do is make love to you all night long." Diana giggles and kisses him and he kisses her so passionately, then kisses all over her body till he gets to her tummy and going further down to her vagina, kissing and licking her clit. Diana pulls his head into her more and starts moaning, "Tony I have missed you so much too. Do whatever you want to me and don't stop my love all night long." Tony happily obliges and climbing on top of her body takes all her clothes off and his own off quickly, and starts to pump inside her slowly at first. Then fast and faster until she is screaming Tony I love you so much, I'm going to come. So he stops, teasing her with his hand and tells her how much he wants her to orgasm. With him too, I think you should go down on me my love and suck me off until we both orgasm together. Diana obliges and screaming orgasm so loudly together again.

Both awake at the same time. Tony turns to Diana and says, "you was magnificent last night my love. I never wanted it to end." Diana says, "me neither Tony I have never been so happy to see you and just wanted it to go on forever and ever." Both looking at each other start kissing again, but unfortunately Tony has to go to work. So Tony leaving Diana horny again, Diana gets her vibrator out and playing with it, pushing it inside her. Thinks of Tony before she orgasms for the last time today.

Diana starts getting dressed and drives to work. Walking into the office, her boss says, "It's nice to see you Diana and am happy to tell you that you have been promoted to assistant manager. I put you in for this position a few months ago, as I was so happy with your commitment to helping young children and babies. I have never seen another social worker care as much as you do. I know you will change the way things are handled around here from now on. Diana feeling very happy with her new role. Starts straight away helping the children and babies, by thinking what can I do to change the way we go about dealing with parents, or other people from hurting vulnerable babies and young children. Well a thought comes to mind, she thinks well I'll remove them from the danger straight away, by putting them into care immediately and getting the police involved.

With that Diana puts stronger rules in place. Feeling happy Diana looking forward to these new rules taking effect from tomorrow. She looks through her list of the most vulnerable. Seeing a new case about a baby, that must have come in while she was off. Seeing that the baby was only 6months old and being severely beaten by mother and her boyfriend. Thought I will go to the house immediately and remove the baby from home to care. She knocks on the door and says where is your baby? The mother says, "My boyfriend has taken her out for the afternoon." Diana finds out where and immediately goes to the park. Seeing a man pushing a baby girl, shouts his name and he turns around. So she goes over and says, "I must take you both home straight away, I will explain when we get there."

Diana drops them both off and goes into the house with them. She quickly rings the police. They come out very quickly as it's an emergency. Diana explained the situation and the police take them both in for questioning. While Diana taking the baby to hospital to be examined, the doctor does a thorough check up and says, "This is the worst condition I've seen a baby in for a long time, she has a broken back, bruises all over her little body! Cigarette marks on her head, which her hair covered up. I say she should be immediately moved from her house. Diana taking the baby to emergency care straight away. Then goes back to the office to write a report and request that baby goes into emergency care. Where she will be safe immediately. Diana rings the police to come out straight away as it is an emergency. Police arrive quickly and Diana tells them everything. The police go back to the station where they do a formal arrest. And with all the evidence they have. The mother and boyfriend go to prison, never to have custody again of sweet little baby Joanne. Diana feeling empowered, goes on to help many babies and young children in her career.

Chapter Eighteen

One night out in Blackpool night club with Graham and Diana is at the bar, and guess who spots her!?! Jim her horrible boyfriend from a long time ago. Diana shouting at him to go away catches Graham by surprise, he goes over to help Diana calm down and the horrible Jim cowardly slips away. By the time Diana explains everything to Graham telling him that he broke her dog Bouncer's back. Graham is so angry for Diana, that he promises, "Jim will know exactly how bouncer felt, like they say. What goes around comes around. And Jim will certainly get what he deserves."

So Graham gets in touch with a few of his mates, and they go to Blackpool and wait outside the night club for Jim, wearing balaclavas and gloves for their baseball bats. Jim comes out and first Graham approaches him and says, "This is for what you did to poor Bouncer!" And with that whacks him around the head, then the other lads come running in and each of them whack his back and head repeatedly. Until Jim is no longer moving. So Graham gets closer to him checking if he is still breathing. Says to the other men, "Jim isn't breathing, we need to get out of here quickly."

Graham getting home. Cannot sleep until he has rang Diana in the morning. Telling Diana exactly what happened, Diana is so happy and just wants to see him straight away. So Graham goes to pick her up as soon as. Taking Diana back to his house and bedroom. Diana says, "thank you Graham, you can do whatever you want to me forever and ever." Graham opening his sex toys drawer says, "Choose which one you want to start with first." Diana points to the large vibrator and with that Graham putting it inside Diana, starts to push it up and down until Diana is moaning so loud and says, "I'm going to come. Graham stops and says, "Oh no you're not my queen, I've not finished with you yet." So Graham kisses Diana all over her body, going further down to her bottom and starts licking in between her cheeks, then turns her over to the front and licking her clit and licks all her cum away. Diana going down on Graham too so they're in the 69 position. Graham screaming I'm going to come. So Diana sucks faster and faster until he comes in her mouth, she then swallows it. Diana doesn't want it to end, so putting a condom on Graham, sits on top of him and starts riding him until they're both screaming. Orgasms together again.

Back to work for Graham and Diana. First thing to do is call Tony and see when he's home. Tony is coming home at the weekend. So Diana rings Graham up to tell him she can stay with him until the weekend. Graham buzzing and feeling very excited to be sleeping with Diana for the next 5 days, thinking I'll book a table at Chickitours, our favourite restaurant and surprise her. Anyway Diana finishes work and goes home to put a few clothes in a suitcase for the week. Then driving to Graham's, they both feeling excited to be spending the next 5 days together. Graham says, "Right we need to get dressed, because I'm taking you to out my love."

So all ready to go, Graham drives them. They have a great time drinking, eating and lots of chatting about when they go to Dubai. The next day after work, Diana feeling excited about her first time going to Dubai, goes on a shopping spree and buys lots of summer clothes. Especially bikini's and sexy beach wear. She buys some crutch less bikini bottoms, which she knows will drive Graham absolutely wild with desire for her and some really sexy revealing bikini bras, she can't wait to show Graham. That evening after they've eaten their tea. Diana says, "Graham I've got a surprise for you!" Then disappeared upstairs to change into her sexy bikinis. Coming back downstairs, strutting across the floor modelling each one sexy and sexually. Driving Graham absolutely wild, he grabs her and throws her to the floor. Saying, "Diana you sexy little kitten, you have no idea how turned on I am right now."

Diana tells Graham, "I can sort of imagine how turned on you are my love." And with that she says, "I'll show you." So she grabs him on the floor and putting a condom on, sits on top of him starts riding him slowly. Then fast and faster until he screams out, fucking hell Diana! "You are amazing! I'm coming my beautiful, sex kitten. You are so good, I could make love to you for the rest of my life."

Chapter Nineteen

Well it's 2023 and Diana and Graham cannot wait to go to Dubai. It's not long to go now. A few weeks and they'll be able to see each other every day for two weeks. Diana feeling a bit guilty about it, but at the same time looking so forward to it. In the meantime it's work for them all. Diana is helping babies and children so much with her new rules. Her manager calls Diana in to give her some positive feedback, about her help so far and says, "You'll be running this place soon." Diana can't wait to tell Tony and her family, when she gets home from work. Diana is also looking forward to seeing Graham, and sharing her good news with him too.

To celebrate, Tony takes all the family out for a nice meal. And Diana lets Gabriel and Cameron choose where they go. Afterwards Cameron has been wanting to watch The Avengers at the pictures, so they all go to watch it. Everyone really enjoys it, even Gabriel who was moaning at first. Diana had to persuade her with lots of treats. It always works, Gabriel takes after her mum for chocolate and cakes. Cameron is like his Dad, they can take them or leave them. Diana so wishes that Gabriel was like them too, because she has such a beautiful figure just like her mum did when she was that age.

Chocolate cake and chocolate in general was definitely the undoing of Diana's beautiful body. She really hoped more than anything in her life. That Gabriel didn't make the same mistake as she did. But the more she preached to Gabriel, Gabriel would just laugh and tell her, to stop worrying so much. But Diana can't help preach to her because she's got such a stunning body and face. Diana thinks she's even more beautiful than herself was, and doesn't want her to throw it all away. And one day look back with so much regrets like Diana does.

It's time for Diana to meet up with Graham, and she can't wait to tell him, her good news. Graham is very happy for Diana and says, "We should go out together to our favourite restaurant for a nice meal my love, my treat beautiful." Diana doesn't have the heart to tell him, no because she's already done that with her family. So she agrees and says, "Yes sounds good." Graham also asks, "Do you fancy going pictures too, "because Spider-Man 3 is on and it's one of my favourite marvel movies." Diana laughing says, "Yea it's one of Cameron's too. You men never grow up do you?" Anyway, they go to the pictures after their meal and Diana thinking to herself it's just like, when me and Tony took the kids out, ha-ha! But didn't say anything. So because it was the weekend and Tony was away from home, Graham says, "Diana would you like to come over to mine tonight? And we can finish the night off in style." So that is exactly what happened.

Monday morning and It's back to work for Diana and Graham. Tony is also home tonight too, giving Diana an idea asked, "Tony should we all go out together again tonight my love. Spider-Man 3 is on at the pictures? Tony delighted says, "Yeah we'll surprise the kids and take them out for a meal first." So Cameron is excited and happily says, "thank you mum and dad, I'm buzzing now. Because all my mates want to go pictures to watch it, but no one can afford to go." Diana feeling really happy that she had found out that it was showing at the pictures. Thinking to herself it does payoff seeing Graham after all, because Tony's not clued up on what marvel movies are out at the moment. So, Diana really does have the best of both worlds, she's just starting to realise it now.

Chapter Twenty

Well Dubai has finally come around and Graham and Diana are so excited to be finally going. Diana says, "Graham it feels like it's come around so fast, but at the same time took a long time to get here. It feels strange doesn't it love." Graham agrees saying, "it does my beautiful, but it will only get better from here now my love."

Well the day is finally here, Diana gets home from work early to do some packing. She has now finished for 4 weeks, feeling excited but also feelings of guilt for Tony. Thinking to herself, I'll surprise him at bedtime. So just before they go up to bed, Diana says, "Tony just give me a few minutes, I've got a surprise for you my love." Going up the stairs, she gets her bikini's out. She bought three of them, black, red and white. She thought to herself the white one will look a lot better, when I have got a tan. So I'll surprise him with that one when I get home. She puts the black one on, crutch less knickers and a very see through, revealing bra. Looking very sexy strutting her stuff, shouts Tony to come in. When Tony sees her he says, "Wow Diana you look very sexual my sexy beautiful wife, I hope you're not planning on doing anything with someone in Dubai, thinking what happens in Dubai, stays in Dubai. No she lies and laughing says, "I would never do anything like that to you love."

Tony can hardly control himself, watching Diana strutting along the floor. Grabs her and picking her up, throws her onto the bed and takes her clothes off and his own very quickly. He pants out, "Diana I love and want you so badly, let me make love to you all night." Diana exclaims, "Tony you don't have to ask love, just do it all night long my sexy beast and take me roughly, because I want you so badly. He doesn't need telling twice. He kisses her so passionately and kisses her body all over again and again, going down on her kissing and licking her clit, he drives her crazy. Diana screaming and crying out, I'm going to come love. So tony taking her roughly from behind pumps and pumping inside her until they are both moaning loudly, they climax together again and again until they are so tired out. They just pass out and sleep until the morning.

Saturday morning they wake up and do it all again. What a lovely time they're having on a Saturday morning, that goes on until the afternoon, all orgasmed out. They get up, shower together and dressed, then they are both ready to go out. Tony bringing the car round they get Leo in first, then he drives to Heaton Park and they walk around with Leo because it's a lovely sunny day. Leo loves his walks, which he gets four times a day. It's a shame they can't let him off his lead though to have a good run around. Because he doesn't come back when you shout him. Leo is very clever. But one thing he can't remember from his training is recall, which is such a shame though, because he would love to just run around, but he can't be trusted to come back when shouted. From a puppy, tony took him to a training club called Wagga cuffs and he was so clever. He would pick everything up so easily. Easier than all the other dogs, but Diana got very ill with chronic fatigue, and was bed bound for 5years. So tony didn't have any time to carry on with his training. Such a shame! Because he would have made a great Assistant dog for Diana, but nether mind. It just wasn't meant to be.

Leo was so intelligent. It was such a shame for him. Because Diana had M.S, Tony hadn't always been able to take him where he wanted to. But now Diana is up and about. They both can take him to nice places when off from work. Especially now they can train him to recall. Tony, Cameron and Diana all take Leo to Heaton Park, which is the biggest park in Europe. Tony puts Leo on a very long lead, so he can go for a little run. Tony and Diana are on one side of the field and Cameron is on the other side, and when Cameron shouts him he runs over so happily, his legs look like they're going everywhere. He looks like a little puppy again so cute, and then Tony shouts him and when Leo goes to him, he gets a treat. Which Leo would do anything for a treat. Tony used to take him swimming lessons at a pool for dogs, he was doing so well. But then the swimming pool had to close down. Due to COVID 19. Poor Leo didn't have much luck. But was lucky to be with Tony, Diana and the kids, because they all love him so much and Gabrielle is always spoiling him. Anyway I'll get back to my packing thought Diana. Because we fly out on Monday at Manchester airport. And Diana and Graham are so excited! They can hardly wait.

Diana getting into her packing, has made a list so she doesn't forget anything. Even though Graham said, "don't worry if you forget anything my love, we'll just buy it over there." So it sort of takes the pressure out of it. Putting the towels in first then building it up, Diana loves packing to go away but hates it coming back home. She puts her sexy underwear in and gets a twinge of excitement thinking about what they'll be doing. Getting quite turned on, she rings Graham to tell him how much she loves him and can't wait to see him. Tony has took Leo out for a walk and Diana feeling horny gets out her vibrator to have a little play while thinking of Graham. It doesn't take long for her to come and come for a few times, then she hears Tony coming in so quickly puts it away. Tony looks at Diana and says, "You look a bit sweaty love are you ok? Diana says, "Yeah I'm just a bit warm love." So Tony replies, "Do you want to do something that will make you really sweat my love, while we've got the house to ourselves, and we can make as much noise as we want." Diana looks at him and says, "I'd love to my love because I'm going to miss you so much." Tony taking Diana to the bed says, "I love you so much and I'm going to miss you like crazy. So let's get a bit crazy now." Diana feeling even hornier now just lies back and enjoys.

Chapter Twenty One

Diana meeting Graham at the bus station as planned is really, really excited. She gets in his car and he kisses her so passionately. Both extremely excited getting to Manchester airport, check in and then feeling more relaxed. Graham buys himself and Diana some drinks. Diana says, "I'll have vodka, lime and lemonade please" She always drinks vodka when flying, it calms her nerves. Diana has always been very scared of flying, but knows that if she wants to get to these Amazing countries, she has to fly.

So now it's time for take-off, Diana's favourite part, she loves the speed. And the adrenaline she gets from it. So up in the air which Diana hates usually, but Graham is making it exciting as he can by kissing her and whispering in her ear, what he is going to be doing to her when they get to Dubai. Diana feeling tingly all over whispers, "Graham I can't wait because you're turning me on so much." Graham whispers should we go to the toilets where I can relieve you a little bit." Diana nodding yes, so Graham whispers, "Diana pretend that you're not feeling well and I will take you to the toilet." So Diana starts acting like she's going to be sick, then Graham holding her hand leads her to the toilet. Once in the toilet Graham grabs Diana pulling her knickers down he licks her clit quickly until she comes and trying to be as quiet as she can.

Well getting back to their seats Diana says. "Well that's the first time on a plane giggling. She whispers "that's taken the boredom away anyway, just wish we could do more." So Graham taking his coat off covers Diana up puts his hand down her knickers and fingers her. Diana closing her eyes is really enjoying it. Then she feels the familiar feeling that she is about to orgasm. So silently whispers, "I'm going to cum" as she can orgasms. She just wants to scream out loud because it's an amazing feeling doing it on a plane. But she resists. Then feeling sleepy rests her head on Graham's lap.

Then she wakes with a startle when she hears a Big Bang, and is thrust back in her seat! In shock she looks around and everyone is panicking. She looks at Graham and he is saying, don't worry we're going to be ok, but his face is looking a bit panicked. The air hostess is telling everyone not to panic. Make sure you are all back in your seats safely and put your seat belts on immediately. Before she sits down and puts her seat belt on. Looking around and outside the window, she sees that one engine has blown on one of the wings. Graham says, "Don't worry Diana, a plane can fly with one wing. Then the pilot comes on the Athena and says, "all passengers stay in your seats and make sure all seat belts are fastened tightly we have lost one wing but can still make it home safely."

Diana still is so scared, she hates flying as it is. Graham trying to be as calm as he can be. Takes hold of Diana's hand and says, "I think we're going to be ok so not to worry my love." Diana's thinking to herself I should have known better, this is my punishment for cheating on Tony. But to be honest she thinks maybe I'm just over panicking because I feel so guilty on Tony and the kids. Then they hear another bang and the plane starts Shuddering! Now Diana is panicking like mad. She says, "Graham I can't cope on this plane, I just want to get off!" Graham says, "don't worry my darling we're going to be fine." But Diana has a bad feeling in her gut.

Chapter Twenty Two

Diana's gut is proving to be right unfortunately. Pilot announces that he's going to have to do an emergency landing, but tells everyone to stay calm and make sure your seatbelt is fastened tightly. The air hostesses are at the front of the plane demonstrating what to do in an emergency. And if we land on water, they all have a life jacket under their seats. Demonstrating what to do with the life jacket. Diana thinks to herself, it doesn't look too complicated. But is still shaking with fear. She is so scared! Graham puts his arm around her trying to calm her down

Well things just get worse and they're all screaming when the plane just drops all of a sudden! It's dropping quickly now! Diana thinks this is it. We're all going to die but then becomes quite calm. Thinking if this is it, I've had a good life overall. Sometimes a bit dramatic but I love my life with my family and friends. I wanted to die a few times in my life. But was so glad I didn't, because things that you think you can't get through. You always do and things do always get better. Have you ever heard that saying, "What doesn't kill you makes you stronger" It's very true so never ever give up, please take it from someone who has been there.

So feeling very sad, starts crying thinking, I will never see Tony, my beautiful children and Leo my Amazing dog. Who to be honest is like one of her children too. Tony and Diana have always treated Leo like family. Him being the baby of the family. As he is only four, I know that makes him 28 years old in our years, but he was treated like a baby, so four years old suited him a lot better. Feeling very emotional as the plane starts dropping faster, Diana starts feeling stronger and feeling more like she can fight this. Thinking to herself if I can survive 5 years being completely bed bound! I can get through anything.

Thinking of her perfect family and how much she loves them makes her not want to give up. So doing exactly what the pilot and Cabin crew had suggested. She gets into the emergency landing position. The pilot announces that they are about to land on the water, so get your life jackets on and say a prayer. Diana prays for herself and everyone on the plane especially Graham to all be ok and make it safely to land.

So feeling a massive thrust and hearing the engines so loud, hit the water. It was such a horrible sound and feeling. Diana looks at Graham and seeing him not moving, shouts out his name as loud as she can! Graham not responding. Diana turns to him and starts nudging him and shouting out his name as loud as she can. So painfully has to move without him and starts making her way to the exit doors. All she can think about is seeing her family again. Going down the security ramp into the freezing cold water. She doesn't feel much only numbness as she looks around and can only see a few people. Then she hears a man's voice shouting this way. So following him quickly, as she's feeling thankful for her life jacket. Swims as fast as she can and doesn't look around. Only focusing on making it to land and being safe thank God!

Diana feeling grateful she's made it to land, she sees the man who is actually the pilot. He's shouting to her and a few other people. Help is on its way. So stay as calm as you possibly can. And we will be rescued, no need to panic. Diana shaking because it was so cold in the sea, looks around and sees other people shaking and crying too. She can't help but think this is her punishment for having an affair with Graham. And that's why he is dead. Then she starts crying, but feeling grateful she has been spared to make it up to Tony and her beautiful family. Feeling more happy now, she can't wait to be rescued and go home to see them all again. She thinks to herself should I admit everything to Tony she thinks it's a good idea and just hopes that he won't leave her and forgive her.

Then she hears a plane and the pilot shouting here's our rescue. Thinking thank goodness but feeling a bit anxious to be going back on a plane. It looks like she's not the only one who is feeling anxious. A woman is screaming I'm not going back on a plane! The pilot goes over to calm her down and says, "I understand how you're feeling, but remember flying is still the safest way to travel, and it's a good idea to get back on a plane so you won't be scared of flying in the future. Trust me I know it's hard. But you need to face your fears and you will be thankful, I don't want you to suffer for my mistakes. Diana wondering what he means by that statement, but all becomes clear later on in the book so carry on reading.

Chapter Twenty Three

Anyway has they are all getting on the plane. The pilot counting everyone, says, "Ten including myself have survived." Everyone started clapping loudly but also feeling sad for all the people and children who didn't make it. The pilot says, "Once we're all on the plane we should say a prayer for all who haven't survived." Diana and the others put their heads down. Feeling very sad especially for the children who didn't make it. Once all on the plane, the pilot announced we will be taking off very soon, so anyone who wants the toilet better go now. So Diana gets up to go to the toilet.

All getting back in their seats and putting their seatbelts on. The pilot announces that everyone should put their hands in the air to pray. So everyone raises their hands up and bows their head, while the pilot starts with the prayer 🙏 at the end everyone says amen. Everyone feeling grateful they have survived. It doesn't seem that long on the plane before the pilot announcement comes back on to say they are landing at Manchester airport. Everyone saying thank goodness. Diana can't wait to get off and see tony. They land and everyone starts clapping very loudly. All getting off and saying thank you to the pilot for getting them home safely. Then Diana spots Tony and running to him, they embrace and Diana hugging him so tightly feels like she never wants to let go.

Waiting in a que to collect some of the things that have been saved. Diana says, "Tony I'm just so happy to be here! I don't care about the things that have been lost. It's just stuff that can be replaced." Tony kisses her and says, "You have no idea how happy I am to have you back home safely." Diana hugs him very tightly and kisses him so much. Thank goodness she is back home, that's all Diana can think about, is when she is back in her house and sees the rest of her family.

Walking through the front door she is greeted by Leo her beautiful dog, who's tail is wagging so fast. Then her children run over and hugs her and kisses her so much. Leo making sure he is not left out jumps up to get closer to them all. Diana laughing says, "Leo you always make sure you are not left out of anything don't you."

Well it's late so Diana just wants to get in bed, she's so tired. So everyone goes to bed and has a good night's sleep. Except Diana! She's tossing and turning and shouting out Graham's name.

When they wake up in the morning, Tony says, "Diana who's Graham? Diana In shock says, "What's made you ask about that name?" Well Tony says, "You have been shouting his name out most of the night and had a very restless sleep my love." Diana goes quiet, then she says, "Tony I'm so sorry I have something to tell you." Taking a deep breath says, "I hope you can forgive me Tony, but I have been having an affair with a man called Graham, I am so sorry, I didn't have to tell you because he died in the plane crash, but I feel so guilty, I was about to go Dubai with him until the plane crashed. I genuinely think that was my punishment for all the lies I told you. I am so sorry Tony but I had to tell you, because I feel so guilty about it." She then goes on to say, "I never stopped loving you, it was just the excitement that I found in him because you was working away so much."

Diana sobbing says, "Can you forgive me Tony?" He sighs and looks down at his feet, "I'm not sure, I need some space from you to think." With that he gets up, dresses and packs a bag Saying, "Tell the kids I have to work away for a few days." And he walks out the door. Diana sobbing can't stop crying and thinking he's going to leave me. What am I going to do without him. I've been so stupid but I had to tell him the truth. She spends the rest of the day in bed and tells Gabrielle and Cameron she's not feeling too good. They ask where is dad? She tells them he's working away for a few days like he told her to say. Then Gabrielle says, "Mum I'm just going to take Leo out for a walk while you rest, Mum you have been through so much! You just need a good rest and then I think you'll be ok."

Diana starts to cry again and feeling more ashamed of herself, finally falls back to sleep. When she awakes Diana checking her phone to see if Tony has rang. Doesn't see any missed calls, so decides to ring him and beg for his forgiveness. Tony doesn't answer, Diana knows he must have seen her calling. And decided not to answer, but Diana is not ready to give up. Despite everything she has done to him she still loves him dearly. So she rings him again and he answers saying, "Diana I have nothing to say to you, I don't forgive you." Diana crying says, "Please Tony I don't want to live without you, I love you so much. Please give me another chance, I'll never let you down again please forgive me." Tony hangs up with never am I going to forgive you Diana.

Chapter Twenty Four

Diana's phone is ringing so she quickly answers it thinking it's Tony. She hears a voice she doesn't recognise asking to speak to Mrs Spencer. Diana says, "Speaking" So the voice says, "My name is Mr Shelter I would just like to offer you a chance to meet one of your favourite famous people, as you was one of the ten people to survive a plane crash." Diana excitedly says, "Oh really I would love to meet Josh Groban. He's my favourite musical Singer and actor, I love him so much and would love to meet him more than anything in the world please." Well Mr. Shelter says, "Can I ask you to come on the T.V show Saturday night with the two brothers." Diana exclaims, "Yes I will thank you so much for that."

Diana is all ready to go on the show, feeling really nervous but so excited too. Looks around and seeing the Pilot stood with a few other people. Goes over and standing with them all. Alan and David come onto the sage telling the story of the plane crash, and how it was down to the Pilot's mis-judgment of Mechanical Issues that caused the crash. So asking first for all the ten people to come on stage. Diana walking out with them all, is feeling so nervous but so excited at the same time. Alan approaches them all and says, "Who would like to go first." The Pilot says, "I'll go first seeing as though it was my fault." Alan nods and says, "I just have a few questions for you before you meet your favourite famous person." Ok says the pilot whose name is John.

John is answering a lot of questions he's having thrown at him and then he meets Eric Clapton his favourite famous person. Alan says, "Who would like to go next?" Diana stepping out so Alan says, "What makes you want to meet Josh Groban?" Diana says, "Because I just love him so much. I first heard him sing on the Christmas film Polar Express, and fell in love with his voice so I searched for him on the internet and since then I have listened to all his songs, my favourite one at the moment is 'Granted' and 'In her eyes' comes a close second. Because it reminds me of myself, if I was ever lucky enough to get close with him! Well I can dream can't I lol. I watched him on Netflix in 'The Good Cop." So says Alan, "David bring Josh Groban out please." Josh Groban walks out and Diana's legs go so weak. He walks over to Diana and taking her hand and bows his head to kiss her on the lips. Diana's having a really good chat with Josh Groban, he's so down to earth and even says, just call me Josh. Diana feeling like she has a strong connection to Josh Groban, and wondering if he feels it too, she looks Josh straight in the eyes and he smiles at her, taking Diana's breath away. And then she has to say good bye walking off the stage with wobbly legs.

Diana is still buzzing when she receives a phone call from Josh Gorman. Asking can he meet her again. Diana exclaims, "Yes of course I would love to meet you." Josh replies, "Can I call to your house now please." Diana feeling so excited shouts out, "yes do you know where I live?" Josh says, "Yes of course I know where you live, I'm outside now." So Diana running to the door to let him in says, "Come on in." Josh Walking In says, "Diana I just feel like I have a connection with you and want to kiss you more." So Diana melting kisses him and hugs him. Bringing him over to her bed says, "I don't know if my husband has left me he won't reply to my phone calls." Josh says, "Can I lie with you for a bit." Diana exclaims, "of course you can" all Josh wants to do is just kiss her. He is so respectful. Diana says, "Josh there's not a lot of men that would be respectful as you're being right now thank you for that. Josh says, "It's because I really like you Diana and I would like to see you again." Diana says, "yeah absolutely Josh I would like that." Josh asking, "What is your life like living here?" So Diana replies, "I love living here, life has not always been easy for me though living with multiple sclerosis." Josh shocked says, "well you look good for it Diana." Diana says, "thank you but you wouldn't have said that if you had seen me ten years ago. I was bed bound for five years due to no fault of my own. I was on a drug for my M.S called Gilenya. While I was on the drug I carried on walking to the Lancashire Racket club, which was about 4miles away. Where I went in the gym for a little bit, done some swimming and went into a Pilates class which I absolutely loved. I loved my life at the time, but my Consultant kept telling me to bring the reins in. But I only did as much as I could. Until I started feeling more fatigued! So I used to rest. Until my fatigue got worse that eventually I became bed bound!" My consultant blamed it on me saying, "I had over done exercising and now I was suffering with Chronic Fatigue. It was the worst time of my life. I just lay there for five years only being able to do minor things, I blamed myself because I had ruined everyone's life. Like my husband Tony who had to do everything that I used to do with the kids and also go out to work. He deserves a medal for everything he used to do, and that's how I repay him by having an affair. Anyway when I finally changed my consultant and came off the drug, my chronic fatigue started to disappear. So life was good again and I could start to relive my life. Until I had a massive M.S relapse and ended up in hospital for six months and 3 months in the Floyd unit, which is a rehabilitation hospital where you go to recover."

So Josh replies saying, "well done Diana you've done so well. You are an inspiration." He pulls her into himself to kiss her more passionately. Diana is getting very excited and tells Josh, "I would love for you to make love to me." But Josh declining says, "I can't do that as much as I would love to. But you are a married woman and I could never destroy a relationship with your husband and lovely family." Diana says, "thank you Josh for putting my family first. There is not a lot of men that would do that in your position right now." Josh says, "Do you think your husband will come back to you?" Diana sighs and says, "I'm not sure he was so angry with me." Josh says, "Can I ask what you did to him?" Diana says, "I cheated on him with a guy called Graham. Who was taking me to Dubai, when the plane crashed, unfortunately he didn't make it." So Josh says, "I am so sorry to hear that. But if you hadn't survived I would never have met you. I'm a true believer in fate, so I believe we were meant to meet. I'm just not sure why, but it will all become clear soon I suspect and hope so. You are very beautiful Diana." Diana says, "Thank you for that, but you are good looking too, and can have anyone you want". So Josh says, "And I just want you." And with that he pulls her closer to him and starts kissing her very nice and gently.

Josh really likes Diana, so asking her, "would I be able to take you out for a nice meal and a drink?" Diana excitedly says, "Yes I would love to go out with you" Josh booked a table at one of the very best restaurants he can find. Diana can't believe this is really happening, Diana's so excited to be going out with him and says, "Josh I really like you and have a really good feeling about us. What do you reckon?" Josh says,

"Diana I had a really good feeling about us from day one." waiting for Josh to pick her up. She hears a knock on the door so jumps up, she answers it and sees Josh stood there with a beautiful bunch of flowers. Josh hands them over to Diana. So she kisses him and thanks him for them. Making their way to the restaurant Josh says, "I like you Diana you intrigue me. I would like to get to know you better." Diana says, "I would love to get to know you more too. I feel a strong connection to you. This feels so good to me. Like I'm getting a second chance, and I really don't want to mess it up." Josh smiles and holding Diana's hand, then brings her hand to his mouth and kisses it.

Chapter Twenty Five

In the restaurant, people are looking and whispering, so Josh standing up says, "Hello everyone, yes it's me, I hope you are all having a good time, and enjoying your meal on this lovely evening?" Diana smiling says, "you're just so nice and polite to people aren't you. Don't you just get fed up with people staring at you." Josh smiles at Diana and takes her breath away. Diana still wishing she was somewhere on her own with him, to kiss and get a lot carried away. Telling Josh what she's thinking he says, "Diana I want you too but we just have to enjoy our time out together. And when we get back to your house, I'll stay over if you want me to." Diana says, "I would love you to Josh do you know how much I love being with you?!? It means everything to me, but I want to do more than just kiss you." I know Josh implies but we can't.

Diana is a bit gutted but totally understands, he is a very decent man who doesn't want to do too much because Diana is married and doesn't want to be the reason they split up. He also worries Diana is just star stuck. And doesn't want to take advantage of that. As much as Diana wants Josh she still loves her husband Tony and everything they have been through together. "But Josh I want you so badly I can't help myself, but I do understand why you can't want me too." Diana not willing to give up, because she wants him so badly says, "Josh can I give you a blow job." Josh says I'd love you to but not sure it would be a good idea. So Diana ignoring him, undoing his pants, starts kissing him and kisses down his body. Until she gets to his penis, taking it into her mouth. Starts sucking slowly, then she can hear him moaning. So sucks faster and he says, "stop Diana because I'm going to come." Diana says, "That's fine" and keeps sucking faster and harder until he's screaming I'm coming! So Diana swallows it and says, "I like the taste of you Josh." Josh grabbing Diana and taking off her knickers kissing her all the way down to her stomach, and starts kissing and licking around her stomach, then further and further down to her clit licking and kissing until Diana is moaning loudly and screaming I'm coming.

Both feeling like they're in heaven, Josh looks at Diana and says, "I'm not complaining Diana but we shouldn't have done that as Amazing as it was. Diana laughing says, "I hope you're not Josh why don't you just give into it and we could be having the time of our lives together." Josh says, "Diana I love the taste of you too. I could stay there all day and pleasure you with my tongue so much." Diana says, "Josh that sounds good I could live with that." Diana not giving up! Says, "Josh I don't want to do anything that you're not happy with but I don't want to also give up, because I want you so badly." Josh explains to Diana and says, "I do want you too but we just need to control ourselves better than you are doing at this moment." Then starts laughing.

Diana says, "Ok I will try harder, I do apologise for acting this way, I am not usually like this and feel very ashamed." Josh seems to understand and says, "Don't worry Diana I do understand and I appreciate you being so honest with me." Diana loves being with Josh so much. She feels like she's gone to heaven and doesn't ever want it to end. Anyway tomorrow she's back at work, so will need to get a good night's sleep. But doesn't want to close her eyes and wake up to her having to say good bye to Josh. And never being able to see him again.

So she thinks, but carry on reading and you will see how all Diana's dreams come true.

Morning comes around so fast and it's time to have to say goodbye to Josh Gorman. He smiles and kisses her good bye. Diana is so gutted to have to say good bye, knowing she'll never see him again. Anyway she turns and walks away. Back at her desk, she is thinking I need to get my head back into work mode. Looking at where she left off with the young children and babies. She's about to do some check- up calls, when her boss comes in and says, "Diana I've just had a very worrying phone call about a baby boy in hospital who has been badly beaten." Diana thinking right we have to act quickly, "How old is he? What are his injuries? And what is his name?" Diana says.

His name is Dylan, he is 8 months old, injuries are very severe. He has a broken back, busted nose and fat lip. 2 black eyes and struggling to breathe. The doctor has classed him as an emergency. Need to get him rehomed as soon as possible. So Diana is on it straight away. She is the best at what she does. So the first thing is to get his parents reported to the police straight away, and get him into emergency care as soon as possible. Doctors say, "this is very similar to Baby P. So this case of the baby will be called Baby D." Diana goes around to the house to take Baby D into emergency care, where she meets the police there and they take the parents away to question them. The only difference to Baby P. Is that Baby D was attacked by mum and dad, and he didn't die fortunately he was close to death, but the doctors at the hospital got to him quickly, and saved his life.

Chapter Twenty Six

Diana gets a letter in the post saying Tony wants a divorce. Diana can't believe it, so she tries to ring Tony. But he's still not answering. Feeling absolutely gutted and can't stop crying. Diana has to tell the kids, that their dad will not be coming back home. Gabrielle and Cameron are both in shock and ask why? Diana has to be honest about Graham. And telling them that he died in the plane crash. Gabrielle says, "Does dad know that Graham died in the plane crash?" Diana explains that she cannot get through to Tony, he is not answering his phone. So Gabrielle rings her dad and he answers straight away. Gabrielle explains that Graham died in the plane crash. But Tony is not bothered he says, "That it doesn't change anything. I can't forgive your mum for cheating on me." Gabrielle starts to cry and begs him to come home, but Tony just keeps telling her no and says, "Darling it is nothing to do with you or Cameron. But I'll never be able to trust your mum again."

Gabrielle running to Cameron tells him everything, and Cameron is so upset too. He goes straight to his mum and says, "Mum why did you cheat on our dad?" Diana says, "I am so sorry son. I didn't mean for this to happen but Graham won me over in the end. He wouldn't take no for an answer but he died in the plane crash. And I didn't want to keep lying to your dad, so I told him everything, and now he can't forgive me, which I can't blame him to be honest. I never stopped loving your dad and will regret it for the rest of my life."

Cameron tells his mum, "I am moving out anyway mum, has nothing to do with you and dad. I'm just renting a house near to college in Birmingham with my mates." Diana feeling very upset asks, "Cameron how are you going to pay for that son?" He explains, "Mum I will be getting a part time job at Tesco in Birmingham, and the money I will be saving on bus and train fares will also go towards paying the rent with my four mates." Dana says, "I'm going to miss you so much Cameron. I hope you will come and visit me?" Cameron says, "of course I will mum. You're not getting rid of me that easily." Diana just hugs him and kisses him says, "I'm going to miss you so much but I'm so proud of you son. You have always been so independent and I knew you would be the first to move out."

Diana still feeling really upset. Then Gabrielle coming home says, "Mum I have something to tell you." Diana says, "You're moving out too joking!" Gabrielle says, "How do you know mum." Diana in shock says, "I was just joking darling. I didn't think you would be moving out as well sweetheart." Diana starts to cry even more sobbing says, "This is the worst day of my life! I can't believe everyone is moving out!" Gabrielle hugs her mum and kisses her saying, "mum this is not forever, I am just doing a house share with some of my university friends and It's closer to university. I'll come and visit at the weekends mum so don't worry. And I'm going to miss Leo so much too." Diana says, "I bet he'll be next to move out with your dad. You know how much he loves him."

Well before you know it, Tony comes around to collect Leo. He walks in and says, "I'm sorry Diana but I'll never be able to trust you again. And Leo has always been closer to me anyway." Diana gives a sad smile and says, "I was expecting it anyway." When Tony walked out with Leo, Diana starts crying and can't believe everyone has gone. But thinking to herself, I probably deserve it anyway. But that doesn't make it any easier.

Anyway back at work, Diana putting everything into Baby D. She makes sure that she does everything in her power to keep the parents away from poor little Dylan. Making sure all paperwork is completed, and Dylan is in the best care. She rings the police to check for any updates on his so called parents. The police inform Diana that Dylan's parents will never ever get rights to have him ever again. Diana is feeling so happy with that decision. She thinks to herself well that's one thing gone right today. But she has no one to celebrate her good news with. Anyway thinking about Josh Gorman. She thinks I wonder if I should let him know that my husband has left me. So ringing his number, Josh answers and Diana can hardly speak. Josh says, "Diana is that you love?" Diana says, "Yes it's me Josh I just wanted to let you know that my husband has left me."

Josh in shock says, "Are you ok Diana?" Diana says, "No I'm not alright to be honest, I've lost everyone who I love and care about. My children have also moved out, nothing to do with me and their dad splitting up though. They have just moved on in college and university. Which I am so proud of them both. And I've lost my dog Leo too, to be honest I expected it as he's always been closer to Tony. Has I've never got over losing Bouncer my dog and soulmate too."

Chapter Twenty Seven

Josh says, "Can I meet up with you and take you out tonight?" Diana happily says, "Yes I would love to go out with you Josh."

Josh finds one of the best restaurants and books a table for two. Josh rings Diana up to tell her he'll be picking her up at 7pm take her out for a meal and drink, and lots of entertainment to cheer her up as best as he can. Diana says, "Josh just seeing you will cheer me up no end. You know how mad I am about you." Josh says, "yes but I didn't know even that would be enough to cheer you up."

Well it's 7pm and Diana hears the door go. So answers the door to see Josh stood there as handsome as ever. Josh pulling her into himself kisses her, so passionately, so Diana pulling him into the house. They both fall onto the sofa, Josh is on top of Diana and is kissing her so passionately. Diana doesn't want to go out she says, "Josh can we just stay here, this will cheer me up the most." Josh smiles and kisses her even more saying, "Whatever makes you the happiest my beautiful." Diana looking at him says, "Josh you have no idea how much I just love being on my own with you have you?" Josh says, "I've got a fairly good idea as you keep telling me lol. And I guess you're going to get your own way then aren't you." Diana replies saying, "I hope so Josh You have no excuse now do you."

Josh looks at Diana and laughing says, "It was never an excuse but I'm not arguing with you because I guess I'll never win." Diana replies, "Yes Josh you're learning, finally. I'm going to get everything I have ever wanted, I am so into you, all I think about is you making love to me." Josh starts to kiss Diana so softly at first then getting more passionate he kisses her harder and Diana is getting very excited and ripping his top off. She kisses him all over his body until Josh is moaning. Oh Diana you excite me so much. Diana thinks I've not even started doing what I want to yet. So pulling Josh more into herself she starts to kiss him all the way down to his pants and undoing his buttons pulls them off. Kisses him all the way down to his penis, then she licks and kisses all the way around his penis. Taking it into her mouth starts sucking it very slowly at first. Until she can hear him breathing heavier. She sucks faster and harder until he's moaning so loudly and shouting I'm so close to coming Diana. Oh wow! I'm going to cum. So Diana sucks faster until he's screaming out I'm coming. Diana swallowing his cum remembers the sweet taste of him. And thinking to herself, he is the third man I've ever loved the taste of their cum. Seeing it as a good sign says, "Josh I love the taste of you." Josh grabs Diana and ripping off her clothes kisses her all over her body, then going further down to her clit he licks very softly. Diana is moaning loudly and grabs his head more quickly and moaning loudly says, "Josh go faster." Josh obliges until she's screaming, I'm coming!

Josh climbing on top of Diana says, "I am going to make love to you now." And slowly placing himself into her vagina pushes himself more into her and kissing her quietly whispers are you ok? Yeah Diana says in a breathless voice, "I love it so much and you can do anything you want to do to me, I'm yours." So Josh starts pumping faster and harder until she starts moaning louder, "I want you so badly I can't believe you are actually making love to me. I've wanted this for so long you know that don't you anyway." I too have wanted you, since the first time I met you and now it's finally happening for us both. Because I am famous, I don't think you realise that I'm just a man, who has needs and wants just like everyone else you know. I also used to fantasise about what I wanted to do to you too.

Diana has to admit she never thought of him fantasising about her or anyone else. She says, "I must admit Josh I didn't think you had to fantasise about anyone. You can have anyone you want." Josh starts laughing and says, "why because I'm famous? See you don't see me has just a man do you? You think just because I'm Josh Gorman I can have anyone I want. But no not at all I am not everyone's cup of tea. I'm not really that good looking, I was a geek growing up and got bullied at school. All the cool kids played football and I sang in the choir. I was a nerdy choirboy who got picked on a lot. Then eventually turned into severe bullying. But I got through it and now look at me! Everyone wants to know me and looks up to me. Girls who looked like you in high school wouldn't give me the time of day or like you say even fancy me. I fantasised about them, that's all I could do."

Josh says, "Diana do you get it now?!?" Diana says, "It's funny because in High school I was also bullied and was a bit of a nerd as well. I wasn't very good looking either. I was very shy and my shyness is the reason I got bullied. When I grew up, I became beautiful and I understand what you mean I became very popular too. All the boys that wouldn't look at me twice back in school. Now all fancied me. Life is so funny isn't it! Maybe that's the reason why we have a connection. We're more alike than we know, what do you think Josh? Josh says, "Maybe, I told you it would all become clear, why we were meant to meet. I am a true believer in fate."

Chapter Twenty Eight

Diana can't stop thinking about what Josh said, and thinking life has it's funny ways, but there's always a reason why people meet. Remember that. There is always a reason for everything. Diana cuddling up to Josh just wants him so much, Josh looks at Diana and says, "You remind me of one of my song's..... 'In her eyes' have you heard it?" Diana replies, "Yes I love that song as well." Josh goes on to say, "I'm going to dedicate it to you from now on, listen to the words, it's just you and me. "Diana can I make love to you all night long?" Josh says. Diana feeling really excited replies, "yes Josh please do." So the fun begins, Josh is still really into it an hour later. Diana can't get enough of him.

Josh lasted for a full hour making love to Diana. No man has ever lasted that long with Diana. Josh brought her to multiple orgasms a few times. Wow! Diana said, "I have never orgasmed so much you are such a good lover, very attentive and passionate. How can you be so good at every-thing. You are just so perfect Josh, I am in complete awe and am definitely falling for you, which scares me a bit because I know how much you could hurt me." Josh says, "Diana I could never hurt you, I just want to spend every night with you. Please say you'll spend all your time with me and love me, that's all I ask of you."

Diana I will always be there for you loving you. I will never hurt you, I care for you too much. Just promise you'll never hurt me. Diana is in complete bliss, "I will never hurt you, and I promise to love you too. I fell for you when I first heard you sing 'Believe' watching Polar Express back in 2010 And I have been mad about you ever since. You have such a beautiful singing voice. Josh says, "They call me the choir boy lol, they say I have the voice of an angel." Diana replies, "Well Josh I definitely agree with that one. You have the best choir voice I've ever heard, I could listen to you for the rest of my life."

Josh says, "Be careful what you wish for because you never know what the future holds." Diana replies, "I do wish to hear your voice every day and night for the rest of my life, because I am in love with you and would love to spend my life with you." Josh replies, "Ok we should get engaged then. I'll propose better than that and get on one knee when I find the perfect ring for you." Diana excitedly replies, "WOW Josh! I don't need the perfect ring. I've got the perfect man with the perfect voice. That's all I need and the answer is a million yes's. I would marry you tomorrow in a white plastic bag, I don't need anything from you. I just want you for ever and ever. And the promise that'll you will always love me and be with me forever." Josh says, "I promise you I will love and always want to be with you every day and night of your life." Josh kisses Diana so passionately and lies her down on the bed, to make mad passionate love to her all night. Diana is filled with emotion and can't help but cry with tears of joy as she orgasms multiple times.

Josh wipes her tears and kisses her eyes and says, "Diana I love you so much. You make me the happiest man in the world. I will promise I'm going to propose to you the right way, no matter what you say. Because I have fallen deeply in love with you and I want the world to see how much I love you. I know not everything is about money, but I want to give you everything that you have ever wanted and dreamed about. Diana says, "Josh you are everything I want and dream about forever and ever."

Chapter Twenty Nine

They finally fall asleep after all their love making, and when they wake up the following morning. Diana says, "Josh did last night really happen? Because I feel like I've died and gone to heaven." Laughing Josh says, "It sure did Diana and I want to do it all again all day long." So kissing her all over her face and body. Kisses her all the way down her legs and back up until he gets to her vagina, then kissing and licking all the way around very slowly till he gets to her clit, Diana pulling his hair and head right into her vagina. He starts to lick faster and harder until she is screaming I'm coming so loudly.

Josh kisses Diana and says, "I could get used to this for the rest of my life, making love to you every morning, afternoon and night is everything I have ever wanted and needed. Diana I must have done something very right in life, to have someone as beautiful as you in my life and bed forever more. I am the luckiest man alive."

Diana is feeling so in love and so very happy. She never thought she would feel this happy again. After her husband Tony divorced her, took Leo and kids moved out. She feels like all her dreams have come true. Thinking to herself, wait until my kids hear this news, they won't be able to believe it! But I hope they are as happy as I am for me. They are Amazing children and I truly believe they will be. When they get over the shock! And don't worry about their dad. Because at the end of the day, he left me and I will always love Tony and really hope he finds someone who he truly deserves too. Because he is an amazing guy and was an amazing husband to me. Diana also thinking to herself, how lucky she has been in life to have two Amazing men who she has loved with all her heart. And thinking about Tony, hopes one day when his anger has gone he will be happy for me.

Diana thinking, I love life, and all the ups and downs it brings. All the people I have loved and lost. And it's a true saying, when you hear saved the best until last. Thinking yes I am very grateful and thankful, for everything I have had in life. I was born to the bested mum in the world, had a good and bad childhood and married my Amazing first husband, and two of the best children I could ever ask for. Also my first dog Bouncer, my soulmate and my 2nd dog Leo who was a family dog loved by us all. Mainly bonded with Garry and the kids, as much as he loved me too. And to be honest I never thought I could love another dog after losing Bouncer, but Leo has a very special way about him. That I couldn't help but love him, just as much as Bouncer in the end. He also taught me that loving two dogs more than anything in the world is ok. Just having a moment, how life can kick you down but how life can also help you too. Because now being with Josh has made my life complete bliss. And Diana couldn't imagine being as happy as she is now.

Chapter Thirty

Anyway the following day, just as she thinks her life couldn't get any better, Josh waking her up with breakfast in bed, the best massage she could wish for. Started on her head, neck, back, bum, back of arms and legs then turning her over to her front kissing her lips, face, eyes, neck down her body Front of arms, legs and vagina, then kissing and licking her clit slowly and fast then faster. Every time Diana goes to pull his head in closer, he grabs her hands, saying, "no, no, no, you don't, just be patient. Good things come to those who wait. Laughing as Diana is moaning stop teasing me and wriggling her body so much. Josh just keeps moving her hands away from his head, until eventually holding her hands as she is moaning even louder now. Starts to scream I can't cope, I am so close. So, Josh stopping climbs on top of her body and pushing himself into her says, "Is this what you want my beautiful, sexy, horny, amazing wife to be. Pushing faster and harder then changing the position, he takes her from behind roughly and pumping really hard and quickly she starts screaming oh fucking hell I'm coming oh yeah oh yea oh fucking Yes! I am coming baby don't ever stop. Then she is shouting again straight away I'm coming again I fucking love you so much, then she's shouting I'm coming again and it seems to last forever and ever. Until panting like mad, can hardly get her breath. Stops and eventually says fucking hell Josh "just when I didn't think you can get any better. You give me the most amazing triple orgasms I've ever had. You are just so amazing. I don't ever want you to stop making love to me." And with that she falls fast asleep.

Diana awakening says, "Josh how long have I been asleep?" Josh replies, "About 5 to 6 hours, I was just watching you sleeping thinking how beautiful you are, and how I'm the luckiest man alive. Just thinking and planning how I'm going to propose to you. I just want to make it so special. As it will be my first and hopefully only marriage in my life." Diana feeling very excited and giddy like a child says, "I cannot believe this is actually happening to me I'm too overwhelmed."

Well Josh says, "I'm just nipping out Diana. I won't be too long. You get some nice rest because you're going to need it my beautiful. Diana trying to get to sleep, but must admit is struggling. All she can think about is what Josh has just said to her. Feeling extremely lucky and so happy for her future. Diana thinks I need to pinch myself to see if I'm really alive. Finally Diana gets to sleep and dreaming about herself and Josh getting married. When she wakes up thinks WOW that seemed so real! She sees it as a good omen, Diana has always believed in her dreams so much. Usually in life Diana's dreams have come true. And she knows in her guts. This is going to come true.

She can't wait for Josh to get back. Just lying there on her own, thinks I'll get my sex toys out because I'm feeling so horny. So that is exactly what she does. Spreading her legs inserts her balls into her vagina. Getting hornier and more excited! Gets her vibrator out and puts the vibrations onto her clit. It drives her absolutely crazy! She's thinking of her amazing husband to be Josh before she orgasms so much, lying there wants to do it all again, wishing Josh was there, but while he's not her sex toys will have to do. She's trying to listen out for Josh because she doesn't want history repeating itself. She would be extremely embarrassed if Josh walked in on her and doesn't think she'd ever get over it.

Josh returned and says, "I hope you're rested because I'm going to make so much love to you. Like nobody has ever done before. Diana lies saying, "yes I'm already for your sexy body. Let me be in complete charge for once." Josh smiles and says, "I'm all yours baby do what-ever you want to me." Diana pushing Josh into a chair and tying his hand around one arm of the chair with one of her tights, then the other hand with her other tights, lying down on the bed spread her legs and putting her large vibrator inside herself. Pushes it fast and starts moaning loud until she is screaming out Josh's name. Josh is getting so excited but can't move, he's just watching and thinking what he's going to do to her when he can get out of the chair. He wants her so badly, then Diana's screaming I'm coming!" Diana says, "Josh you're in control now take me however you want." Josh grabs her legs and spreading them out wide, licks all her come and turns her over on her front and fucks her so hard and fast from behind, it's not that long until they both climax together. Josh when he gets his breath back says, "Let's go and shower together my Beautiful."

In the shower Josh getting on one knee, telling Diana how much he loves her Says, "Diana Will you marry me," putting a beautiful ring on her finger on left hand." Diana exclaims excitedly says, "yes of course I will Josh it would be my honour to marry you." So, Josh kisses her so passionately and starts making love to her slowly at first until he is getting so excited Starts pumping inside her faster and with a big scream ejaculates inside her. Diana is just so orgasmed out. And both feeling so relaxed and happy. Josh says, "Would you like to go out somewhere to celebrate our engagement?" Diana says,

"Yes I would love that." So both getting dressed, Josh brings the car round and he takes her to somewhere they can eat, drink and party.

Josh stands up and announces to everyone, "She said yes! All your drinks are on us. And then he says to the barman. Here's my credit card, take it and open the bar to everyone for the night, and bring me a bottle of your best champagne in the house, we are celebrating all night long. This beautiful woman called Diana has made me the happiest man alive! I want the World to know, I am Josh Gorman and I will be marrying Diana the most beautiful woman in the World. So we are celebrating until closing time." Everyone starts clapping and whistling, and shout out, A Massive Congratulations to you both and hope you will be very happy together forever. Josh standing up says, "Thank you everyone we really appreciate it." And grabbing Diana kisses her and then whirls her around the dance floor. Diana laughing has never been so happy!

Printed in Great Britain
by Amazon

17899236R00068